AN
UPRISING
IN ROME

AN UPRISING IN ROME

1849

A Historical Novel

by
RICHARD F. NOVAK

Also by Richard F Novak

Topping the Dome
Adelaide Johnson's Portrait Monument (with Catherine Novak Davidson)
The Platonia Chamber
The Redemptive Scroll

Richard F Novak/SW publishing
toppingthedome.com
Rockford, IL

Publisher's Note: This is a work of historical fiction.

Cover by Alaina Chanel Moore

An Uprising In Rome/ Richard F Novak. 1st ed. 2019

ISBN 978-0-578-48731-1

For my family

Without country you have neither name, token voice, nor rights, no admission as brothers into the fellowship of the Peoples. You are the bastards of Humanity. Soldiers without a banner, Israelites among the nations, you will find neither faith nor protection; none will be sureties for you. Do not beguile yourselves with the hope of emancipation from unjust social conditions if you do not first conquer a Country yourselves.

—Giuseppe Mazzini

Contents

Preface

In 1831, after an underground network called Carbonari failed to start a revolution in central Italy the writer and political activist Giuseppe Mazzini formed a new secret society, *La Giovine Italia* or Young Italy. Its purpose—to continue the campaign for unification of Italy, the peninsula comprising multiple independent kingdoms of which the largest were the Papal States, the Grand Duchy of Tuscany, the Two Sicilies, Lombardy-Venetia, and Sardinia.

In 1834, Mazzini, joined by the fearless warrior and future Italian general Giuseppe Garibaldi, planned a revolt in the city of Genoa and the Piedmont region of northwest Italy. Betrayed by one of Mazzini's close companions, the short-lived revolt was a failure.

Mazzini fled to Switzerland before settling in England where he continued to write his seditious ideology. These books and pamphlets were smuggled into Italy and distributed among the Young Italy groups that had expanded throughout the peninsula.

Garibaldi, sentenced to death in absentia, had also escaped, first to France and then to South America where he became a feared mercenary in both Brazil and Uruguay.

Neither man had abandoned hope of returning to their homeland to participate in a final campaign to unify Italy.

With the death of Pope Gregory XVI in June 1846, Mazzini sensed it was time to expand the work of Young Italy. The ultraconservative Gregory had ruled for fifteen years and rejected any modern innovations or change. Anyone disagreeing with his autocratic reign had been imprisoned.

Into this climate of fear and little hope for progress in the lives of the people of the Papal States a new pope, Pius IX was elected on June 16, 1846. Would the new pope continue Gregory's policies? The people of the Papal States and Young Italy anxiously awaited the answer.

CHAPTER ONE

The Prisoner

T he large crowd surprised Charles when he stepped out onto the street. When he had taken possession of his new studio earlier, the street had been empty. Now, on this hot July afternoon Romans fresh from their afternoon *riposo* or siesta filled Via Sistina. Some gathered in groups of three or four engaged in animated conversation. Others were reading what looked like an official proclamation posted on the wall down the street. Whatever it said, Charles knew it must be important to cause such a commotion.

He made his way toward the cluster of people facing the poster and nudged between the excited Romans pushing, shoving, and stretching their necks to get a better view of the notice. When close enough to read it he saw an official proclamation from the new pope, Pius IX, or Pio Nono as the Italians called him. Dated July 16, 1846, it announced an amnesty for all the political prisoners of the recently deceased Pope Gregory XVI.

This unexpected good news came as a shock for everyone. An American expatriate in Rome, Charles paid little attention to its politics, but a year ago a friend and fellow sculpture student had disappeared.

Almost certainly Piero was in one of Gregory's prisons, but he never had been able to discover where or why. Now, Charles felt he might see his friend again.

He needed to know more and decided to he head for the Caffé Greco, unofficial headquarters of the artists of Rome and an unrivaled place to hear the latest gossip. Perhaps someone there knew more about the released prisoners.

It had been a year since he had arrived in this city with its awe-inspiring ancient ruins scattered everywhere and galleries full of spectacular paintings and sculpture. Aside from the perplexing politics, an incongruity still puzzled him: this feast for the eyes existed in a maze of narrow, dirty, garbage-strewn streets where naked children played, urinated, and worse.

In warm weather people spent their entire day in the streets. The mannerisms of a typical Roman were dramatic, and all conversation embellished and delivered with exaggerated histrionics.

Intermixed with this conflict of the senses were mothers sitting on benches breastfeeding their children or young lovers, arm in arm on the edges of fountains kissing, reinforcing the reputation of a 'romantic' city. Romans offered no excuses for this striking contrast of the spectacular, repugnant, and romantic. After all, no other city in the world could match its history and treasures.

By comparison Charles's home of Washington, the capital of the United States, had few monuments, no art galleries, plain churches, and a puritanical culture. Comparing ancient Rome to adolescent America was impossible, but it wasn't necessary: he couldn't think of a better place to be a sculptor.

He headed up Via Sistina to the top of the Spanish Steps. More beggars, vendors, and tourists than usual crowded the famous ascent to Trinita dei Monti church. This opening proclamation of Pio Nono—perhaps opening salvo would be more appropriate—had sparked a celebration throughout the city. He wove his way down the steps, and across the Piazza di Spagna to the Via dei Condotti and the Caffé Greco.

When he opened the door, the boisterous voices indicated a full house, which was unusual for this time of day. All the seats were occupied and he hoped he hadn't missed the best of the witty conversation and gossip. Men standing between the tables bathed in thick cigar and pipe smoke made it difficult to see. Charles spotted his friends deep in conversation in the second of the three rooms of the cafe. They didn't notice him as he approached and jostled the chair of his good friend William Smyth.

At first annoyed, Smyth turned around, looked up, and recognizing Charles smiled and said, "Charles, where have you been? We've been here at least two hours. Have you heard the news?"

"I was busy moving, but I did. I read Pio Nono's proclamation. It's hard to believe all Gregory's political prisoners will be released."

"But it's true, and everyone is celebrating. Sit down and join us."

Finding a chair in the crowded room took time, but he managed, and grabbed an empty cup from another table. Smyth, a painter from London, and Everett Brown, a fellow American sculptor had all come to Rome around the same time. Good-humored and a serious student of Roman history and architecture, Smyth had introduced Charles to the ancient ruins of the city and the art treasures hidden in the smaller churches.

Brown, a Harvard-educated intellectual from a wealthy Boston family spent most of his time reading and discussing philosophy and politics with whoever would listen. It was a running joke that he'd actually come to Rome to teach the classics.

Charles meanwhile, concentrated on his training and development as a sculptor. Although he admired the wide range of interests of his two friends and mentors he couldn't afford the luxury of any other pursuits, although he admired the wide range of interests of his two friends and mentors.

His family hadn't possessed the means to allow him to continue school beyond the sixth grade, and before coming to Rome he had worked as an apprentice wood carver and then a stonemason.

Filling Charles's cup with wine, Smyth asked, "Did you finish moving? You know we would have been there to help, but this sudden proclamation from Pio Nono demanded our immediate attention." Laughing, Brown nodded his agreement.

"Yes, I managed. My landlord provided me with a cart and a young boy to help. I don't have many things and I'm finished, no thanks to you. By now I know you enough to realize you both despise common labor. Last week when I mentioned the move your dead silence made it clear you had no intention of helping me," replied Charles. "Now, tell me about all this excitement over the prisoner release."

"This changes the political landscape of the city," began Brown as Smyth rolled his eyes and poured himself more wine. "There has been no continuation of the suppression of freedom by Pio Nono. Unlike Gregory, Pio Nono is loved by the people. I guess that's why I feel excited and optimistic about what may happen in Rome."

"My best friend Piero Cifaldi, a sculptor I met when I first arrived in the city may be among the prisoners released," said Charles. "He began his training at Professor Morretti's studio about six months before me. A rebel if ever there was one he never concealed his dislike for Gregory and his policies, but new to Rome I didn't realize how serious that could be. We became close friends when he let me stay with him for the first three months I was here. I'll never forget his generosity. He had little, but he shared it all with me until I received my money from home. Otherwise, I don't know how I'd have survived.

"Then one day he didn't return to Morretti's studio. That wasn't like him because Before that, he never missed a day and I never saw him again. When I asked his friends in the cafe, they would only shrug their shoulders and walk away pretending ignorance. Finally, one day I stopped one of his friends on the street and he reluctantly told me they had arrested Piero."

"Did you ever hear any more about him?" asked Brown.

"No. But that's when this naïve American began his education in the subtleties of Roman politics," said Charles.

"What do you mean?" asked Smyth.

"We're not Romans. That's why we're not invited to join their political discussions," said Charles. "I've said nothing about this before because Piero warned me Gregory had spies everywhere, including this café. Several other friends of his also disappeared. Spies in a cafe, artists vanishing because of their political beliefs. It would never happen at home and I had no desire to join them."

"The Romans surrounded themselves with an invisible wall of silence during Gregory's papacy and I've had little success penetrating it. Over the centuries they've learned to keep their political propensities to themselves during periods of repression," said Brown.

"I've had the same experience," said Smyth. "It's the reason for the excitement today. They like Pio Nono. We've heard that after the proclamation was posted they gathered in the front of the Quirinale, the pope's residence, and wouldn't leave until he made an appearance."

"This fascinates me," said Brown. "Charles do you think you can find Cifaldi?"

"I had no luck finding him when he first disappeared and wouldn't know where to start," replied Charles. "But I hope he's one of the released prisoners. I'll never forget how he helped me and now it may be my turn to return the favor."

"Were you ever part of Cifaldi's political discussions?" asked Smyth.

"No. He taught me a great deal when I started my apprenticeship, and for that I'm grateful. I only remember him mentioning a man called Mazzini one night when we were with his friends here," said Charles. "When Piero mentioned that name it caused an immediate awkward silence at the table until the others, all Romans, changed the subject. There were many nights when Piero went out alone and wouldn't come home until late. He never mentioned where he'd been, and I never asked."

"Mazzini has been writing revolutionary literature for years. That would be a good place for me to understand what's happening in

Roman and Italian politics," said Brown. "Let me talk to our American consul in Rome, James Winton, who follows the ever-changing politics of this peninsula and its kingdoms."

"I've been here for hours," said Smyth. "It's time to go home. I missed my *riposo* today, and the wine is making me sleepy." The others agreed, and left the café together, each heading in different directions.

Walking back to his studio, Charles considered the discussion at the café. He had come to Rome to study sculpture and make it his profession. Politics never interested him, particularly those of a foreign country, and did not see how it could contribute to his success.

Smyth had already sold many paintings to English tourists. Brown never seemed to worry about money. His wealthy family wouldn't let him go hungry. But Charles had rent to pay and his first commission. When he reached his studio, opened the door, and stepped inside, he looked around and felt a sense of pride and accomplishment. With his apprenticeship at Professor Moretti's studio completed and work on his first commission about to begin, he couldn't afford any distractions.

The next morning, filled with creative energy and eager to begin work, Charles unpacked his tools. They were all he owned except for his clothes and the clay model or maquette of his first commission. Removing the damp cloth keeping the clay of his maquette from drying, he inspected its surface and found no damage.

In a separate room a straw mattress for a bed with a table and two chairs left behind by the previous renter, completed his first studio and household. As meager as this was, for Charles it represented a momentous step in his life and career.

Everything else he created over the past year had to remain at Moretti's studio. This would be the only example of his work he had to show visitors to his studio. Rome had many sculptors competing for the business of the hundreds of tourists searching for art. To compete for commissions, he needed a new body of work.

At least that's the way he felt. A block of marble to carve would definitely help dissipate some of this creative energy, and that's exactly where he planned to head next. For the first time it would be up to him to decide which block to choose, causing a brief sense of insecurity. In the past, they had made all those decisions for him in Moretti's studio. His first client had given him the usual half-down payment up front. With no reserves, mistakes took on costly consequences never considered by an apprentice.

The marble yards were across the Tiber River in the Trastevere section of Rome, a long, but welcome walk on this summer morning. People, eager to complete their business or shopping before the afternoon heat filled the streets. Trastevere contained the workshops of hundreds of craftsmen plying their trades. They could be watched through the open fronts of their shops making anything from fine jewelry to cannons. Charles often lingered here for hours wandering through the streets, always learning something new about tools or materials.

Today though, nothing would distract him from his mission. He needed a marble block at least a meter and a half square. Upon reaching the marble yard he began his inspection of the blocks that looked suitable for his commission. It took a while before he found one the appropriate size and shape. While examining the surface, a man approached.

"You look like you found what you're looking for," said the man.

"Yes, I think this is what I need," answered Charles.

From that point on the man dominated the conversation, assuring him he had selected one of the finest blocks of marble in his yard. Dealing with Roman merchants always left him disconcerted. When foreigners in this ancient city had time to reflect on their purchases they were unsure how they had been led from point A to point B. Centuries of negotiating experience gave locals a distinct advantage.

Roman merchants could, as required, exude charm from every pore in their body. Even though the suspicion they were paying too much lingered in the back of their customer's mind, at the end of any negotiation they would have the utmost confidence they were working with an expert who could be trusted.

Charles had good reason for concern. He had never made such a large purchase, and if a defect lay hidden deep within this block of marble he didn't have enough money to buy another and make any profit on the commission.

He wanted to conclude this business as quickly as possible. The longer the marble merchant talked the more uneasy he became, so he agreed to the purchase. Fortunately, the price was within his budget and after discussing the details of delivery, he was on his way back to his studio.

Walking back, he didn't linger to observe any craftsmen. He'd never spent so much money and could only think of the problems that might develop with this first commission.

Approaching the studio Charles was shocked to see a man sitting outside the door. It took him a moment, but eventually he recognized the unshaven, dirty man dressed in rags.

"Piero, I thought I'd never see you again," said Charles, rushing to help him up, and embracing him.

"And I thought I would never see anyone again," answered Piero.

"You're here because of the release of the prisoners?"

"With all the bitterness he could gather, Piero replied, "They set me free yesterday along with all of Gregory's so-called enemies. They weren't wrong. We hated the man. Our only regret is we never had the opportunity to destroy him. He cheated us by dying."

"How did you find me?"

"Wandering through the city aimlessly, I saw one of Moretti's carvers. He told me where you had moved."

"Come in, come in." Charles put his arm around Piero and helped him into the studio. "You must be hungry? Let me get you something to eat and drink. Here, sit down." He brought him a chair and then found some bread, wine, and cheese.

He watched as Piero devoured the bread and cheese washing it down with long swallows of wine. His friend had lost so much weight. He remembered a young man dark, handsome, and full of life, someone he envied because of his good looks and outgoing personality. Now, he hardly recognized the drawn face with the shiny, thin, fragile-looking skin so taut over his cheekbones it looked as if they might break through any minute. The filthy shredded rags covering his body smelled awful.

When Piero finished eating Charles asked, "Have you been in a prison here in Rome?"

"Yes, I've been in the Castel Sant' Angelo prison since they arrested me, I think about twelve months ago. I'm not certain, I lost track of time."

"Were any of your friends with you?"

"No, I knew no one in my large cell. There were twenty of us in the cell."

"What was your crime?"

"I was told nothing, but I had never disguised my opposition to the government of Gregory. One night they broke into my studio, smashed the furniture, tore up my drawings, and dragged me off to prison. I committed no crime. Any hint you either disagreed with him or talked of change and you were arrested. No trial, no notification to your family. You disappeared and if Pio Nono had not granted this clemency, I would have been left there to die. Left to die with nineteen others. Left to die in a rat-infested cell with a floor covered with piss-soaked straw and a stench that made it difficult to breathe."

Charles shuddered when he heard this, paused and said, "Where did you stay last night?"

"I slept on the street. I have nowhere to go. They took all my possessions. I stopped at my studio, or what was once my studio.

Everything's gone. All this because of the great holy man, Pope Gregory." With this the disheveled and bewildered Piero bent forward in his chair, cupped his hands over his face and sobbed softly.

Charles knew it was time to stop questioning him. Left alone, he thought Piero might begin to shed some of this anguish. This would probably be only the beginning of ridding his soul of such horror.

He continued to weep for at least five minutes. When he regained control over his emotions, Charles said, "I want you to take off your clothes so I can burn them. I'll find you new ones. Wash yourself in that basin over there and then you're going to go to my bedroom and sleep."

"I can't impose on you like that. I'll go back out on the street and somehow find a new beginning. I thought you'd be willing give me some clay and a few tools. I know I can carve again. I dreamed of so many sculptures all those months. Those dreams kept me going."

"Let's talk about that after you get some uninterrupted sleep," said Charles. "I insist."

It didn't take much more convincing to get Piero to bed.

Everett Brown was on a mission to discover more about Mazzini. As he drank his morning coffee at the local trattoria he decided the man who could get him the answers he wanted was his friend James Winton, the American Consul in Rome. He ordered another cup of espresso, gulped it down in one quick motion, and headed for Winton's residence.

Winton and Brown had studied together at Harvard College in Cambridge. Anyone who met Brown, no matter where, or on what occasion, would eventually find the conversation, often out of context, included a reference or story about his days at Harvard. Visiting with a fellow Harvard alumnus, was always a highlight of Brown's day.

He was in luck. He found Winton at home working in his office. A short, handsome man about three years older than his friend, he looked up from his cluttered desk as Brown entered and said, "Everett,

I wasn't expecting you today. To what do I owe this good fortune? Sit down, please, sit down."

"Something came up last night at the Café Greco and I thought you might know more about it."

"That's no surprise. Anything can be expected at the café. What was the topic of discussion last night? I have a suspicion what interested everyone at the tables."

"As you surmised all the talk was about the release of the political prisoners. It turns out Charles Grimes was befriended by an Italian sculptor who disappeared about twelve months ago. Charles assumes he was one of Gregory's prisoners."

"There must have been several hundred scattered throughout the Papal States. If you think I can help you find this sculptor, forget it. Pio Nono probably doesn't even have a complete list of the names."

"No, that's not why I'm here. During the conversation Charles recalled his friend mentioned the name Mazzini. I'm here to find out more about him."

"Mazzini. Any Roman having anything to do with Mazzini or his writings would be immediately jailed by Gregory. That's probably what put Charles's friend in prison."

"Merely mentioning the name could get you imprisoned?"

Winton nodded. "Gregory considered any tie to Mazzini or his ideas anathema to the Holy See. He was, and still is, an active revolutionary, bound and determined to bring about his dream of unification of Italy's independent kingdoms. I'm told he's using a secret society to expedite his plan."

"Is there one in Rome?"

"Yes, it's called Young Italy. There's probably more than one secret society in Rome, but that one is the personal conduit for Mazzini's personal revolutionary ideology. Pamphlets are continually smuggled to its members. Anyone caught with one during Gregory's rule was jailed immediately. Perhaps that's what happened to Charles's friend. Mazzini's writings and exploits are complex. He's a complicated man."

"Have you read any of his work?"

"A diplomat from the British embassy showed me two pamphlets they had intercepted and translated. Brilliantly written, Mazzini never deviated from his message, the unification of Italy, but also emphasizes his belief in humanism and the value of each individual in society."

"Does Pio Nono tolerate this organization Young Italy?'

"I don't know. I'm certain he's aware it exists as did Gregory. He released all of Gregory's prisoners, even though many were probably members of Young Italy, so he must not consider the secret society a threat. I've seen no evidence he'll tolerate or recognize Young Italy in Rome."

"I hope Charles can find his friend. I'd be interested to hear more about this secret society, Young Italy," said Brown.

"As would I," said Winton. "But come, I'm tired of working and it's mid-day. Let's have something to eat."

Piero slept for twenty-four hours giving Charles time to find clothes for his unexpected guest. His clothes would never fit his emaciated friend. It also gave him time to wonder why Piero was in prison. Yes, as Piero had said, it didn't take more than a suspicion someone opposed Gregory to end up in prison, but perhaps he did more? He needed to know the full story.

Piero eventually emerged from the back room of the studio as Charles worked on the maquette of his commission. He needed to occupy himself until the marble block arrived.

"*Buongiorno* Charles," said Piero, who still looked haggard, but rested and almost recognizable in the clothes Charles had left for him. "I found these and assumed they were for me. Are they?"

Charles nodded. "That's the best I could do. You look much better. You slept so soundly, I doubt anything could have woke you up."

"These feel like the robes of a prince after what I wore for the past year. I'll pay you back as soon as I can."

"Don't worry about that, I'm returning a favor I never forgot."

"What are you working on? It looks interesting. Have you finished studying with Morretti?".

"Yes, and this is my first commission. My first paying job. How about that?" said Charles proudly.

"I was ahead of you in my work at Morretti's studio. Now you're finished and I've lost at least an entire year of my life because of a tyrant posing as a cleric, the chief cleric," said Piero. "I'm happy for you, my friend. Tell me more about this commission."

"I will, but first I must have a coffee. Let me walk over to the tratorria and have them bring us two. I'll be right back," said Charles.

Piero took the time alone to look around the studio. He picked up the tools, one by one, turning them over in his hands. Then he looked over Charles's clay maquette, a work much more sophisticated than he remembered of his previous work. Charles had matured as a sculptor. He was happy for his friend.

Then Charles returned with a loaf of bread under his arm, followed by a young boy with two coffees on a tray.

"Come, let's sit down at my humble table and have some bread and coffee," said Charles who, as he spoke, noticed a fleeting emotional twinge pass over Piero's face as his eyes became veiled with suppressed tears. He said no more giving him time to compose himself

After a pause Piero said, "Forgive me. This is such a shock. Being free to sit like this and do something that was once routine. I haven't had coffee since they put me in prison. The horror hasn't left, and probably will not fade from my memory anytime soon. But that's enough gloom for today. Now tell me about this elegant maquette."

"I have James Winton, the American Consul in Rome, to thank for this commission. I was finishing my last month with Morretti when Winton sent some tourists to see his work. Ordinarily Morretti would have never given me a chance to show my work to visitors, but I guess he decided to reward me with my apprenticeship almost finished. It's for a family who live in Massachusetts in America.," said Charles.

"It doesn't matter how you get the work, does it?"

"They wanted something to remember a daughter they lost. It's not for the cemetery. They wanted it for the entryway of their home. I decided on this young girl sitting at the edge of a pond, running her hands through the water. They liked the sensitivity of the idea. That's how they remembered their daughter, sweet and gentle."

"I'm sure they'll be happy with the sculpture. You can't imagine how good this coffee tastes after a year of only foul water to drink. Oh, how I missed talking about sculpture."

"It's time to begin your life where you left off."

"I doubt if I can. The wounds are too deep. The hate I felt all that year in prison is now embedded in my soul like an iron stake driven deep into a thick oak tree. How do I pull it out, get rid of it? I can only think of one way. Destroy those who tried so hard to destroy me."

"Won't the police be watching you?"

"Probably, but I can't continue to live in this Papal State that refuses to allow its people to improve their lives. That's not my idea of living. Now, that I've paid such a heavy price for dreaming of a better Italy, why abandon the struggle. I'm more determined than ever. I was a revolutionary before they seized me and after a year in prison I remain a revolutionary, a more passionate one. If they think they broke my spirit, they're mistaken."

"What about your study of sculpture? You were the most talented student in Morretti's studio."

"That can wait."

"So that was your only crime–supporting the overthrow of Pope Gregory. Nothing else?"

"Nothing else. That was certainly more than enough.".

A commotion in the narrow street outside interrupted their conversation.

"What's that?"

"I'm not sure," said Charles as he moved toward the large door of the studio. When he pulled it open he found a team of eight oxen hitched to

16

a wooden sled loaded with his marble block. "I didn't expect this block to be here so soon, but that's perfect. I can begin carving ahead of schedule."

During all the excitement over the next three hours it took to move the marble block into the studio, Charles didn't notice Piero leave.

Rested, in decent clothes, and fueled by his first cup of coffee in a year, Piero headed to where he thought he might find his former comrades of Young Italy. That is, if any had survived. The ability to once again walk the streets of Rome as a free man was both exhilarating, and at times, intimidating. But an unbearable thought lingered. The police might stop and seize him at any moment. Was he dreaming?

His group of Young Italians usually met in a building about half way between Charles's, new studio and Professor Moretti's. Piero walked down Via Sistina toward the Piazza Barberini. Crossing the Piazza, he took a moment to admire Bernini's fountain, *Fontana del Tritone* with the god Triton holding a shell to his lips, and then turned into a side street. Their meetings were held on this street, but he wasn't sure he'd remember which building.

The street hadn't changed, but when he recognized the building, he thought it best to walk past and farther down the street, before stopping to look back to see if he recognized anyone or if anyone followed him. This uneasiness made him hesitate longer than he planned before approaching the building. He even considered leaving. After all, this past year of horror had its roots here.

Then, the door of a building back up the street opened, and out stepped the only woman in his former Young Italy group, Maria. Piero admired her, as did all the members of the group, the secret society planning a revolution with a woman member. Unheard of in Italy. She was special, thought Pero.

About the same age as he, and still as pretty as he remembered, Maria showed no signs of having been in prison. Like Piero, she came from a village in the same mountain area of central Italy south of Rome. He never asked her the name of her village, but assumed it differed little from his, another pocket of poverty-stricken peasants bound to the unproductive mountain soil. How she had broken away from her family and now lived by herself in Rome remained a mystery. Italian women had little to say about their role and destiny in life. Somehow, she had escaped that tradition, but it was unlikely she would ever be welcomed home again.

Maria turned right toward the Piazza Barberini. He waited to see if anyone else left the building or followed her. No one did, and he hurried and followed a short distance behind her. When she turned east on Via Barberini and approached a narrow side street he caught up to her and grabbed her arm.

Maria reacted immediately, pulling her arm away and looking back in anger at the stranger tugging at her. About to shout out, she suddenly stopped. It took her a moment, but when she recognized Piero she let him lead her into a side street.

They continued down the street until they found a building with a deep-set, covered entryway where they could slip out of sight of the people passing. Maria threw her arms around Piero and wept softly as she held him tight.

Kissing him repeatedly on both cheeks she said, "Piero, Piero, you've been released. How wonderful."

"Yes, I have a hard time believing it myself," said Piero. "I can't believe I found you."

"And I you. You're so thin. Where are you staying? You're not sick, are you?"

"Too many questions at once. Your kisses and concern bring back something absent, something taken from my life this past year. Thank you, thank you, now I know I must not be dreaming or delirious."

Maria embraced him once more, not releasing him from her arms for a long time. When she finally let go, she noticed the tears in his eyes, and asked him again, "Where are you staying?"

"With a good friend, an American, Charles Grimes. Do you remember me talking about him? A fellow student I met in Morretti's studio."

She shrugged, "Vaguely. I'm certain I can find you a place to stay with one of our group."

"No, I want to stay with Charles for a while. Perhaps later. Were others in our group seized?"

"Our group of twelve was reduced to six by Gregory."

"Have they all been released?"

"You are the third I know of, but it has only been two days since the release of the prisoners. Sadly, two died in prison, Luigi and Giuseppe."

"How do you know that?"

"Donatangelo was told this by other prisoners who were released."

"Now we have martyrs to avenge. I'll never cease to fight until we unite Italy and destroy the Vatican," said Piero, pounding his fist into the wall.

"We can only hope Giovanni is still alive. I've been walking the streets hoping to find you two. I've not heard anything about him."

"Does the same group still meet?"

"Yes," we've changed locations several times, but we're back on the street where you found me this morning."

"That's not the building where we used to meet."

"No, it isn't, but it's been safe. Will you be coming back to meet with Donatangelo and the group?"

"He's still the group leader?".

"Yes, he's even more active in Young Italy. He's one of the leaders in Rome."

"The sooner I become active in Young Italy again, the better. When's the next meeting?"

"Not for another week, but I'm certain Donatangelo would like to see you before then. Tell me where you're staying and I'll get a time and place for you two to meet."

"Charles's studio is on Via Sistina about half way up the hill from Trinita dei Monti. He moved in only a few days ago, so he has no marker outside. I'll cut a small 'X' into the right lower corner of the door."

"As soon as I arrange a convenient time, I'll come to the studio to let you know," said Maria.

"*Ciao* Maria," said Piero as he kissed her on each cheek before they went their separate ways.

When Piero returned to the studio, he found Charles carving, and startled him when he came up behind him and said, "Already working?"

"You surprised me. I hadn't noticed you left this morning," said Charles.

"I knew I couldn't help moving the block. Getting cleaned up and wearing new clothes returned some of my self-confidence. I had to see if I could again walk about the city without fear of the police seizing me."

"How did it go?"

"I'm overwhelmed, and intimidated in a crowded street, but I hope that changes."

"It will. You've only been free for forty-eight hours. Did you see any of your friends?"

"No, I saw no one. How's the marble carving?"

"With ease. I think I have a good block. My chisel cuts through the marble with minimal effort. What a nice feeling."

"I miss that feeling. I'd like to try working with clay again. Perhaps in a day or two I can see if I still have any sculptural skills left."

"I'm certain you do. Do you think you're up to visiting the Caffé Greco tonight?"

"This sudden change in my life tires me. I need rest. Perhaps tomorrow night would be better," said Piero.

"Fine, tomorrow night," said Charles who resumed his carving and Piero went to lie down in the next room. He slept through the rest of the day and night.

CHAPTER TWO

Young Italy

At sunrise, the cool morning air welcomed Piero to a marvelous new day. For the first time since his release he felt like a free man. Charles still slept and Piero didn't wish to disturb him. He poured water into a basin and washed his face and hands. The routines of normal life had begun. He looked for something to eat and found bread, olive oil, and a few onions, the basic staples of peasant life, that today were as appealing as a king's feast. After savoring his first morning meal without having to compete for scraps of food with nineteen other starving cellmates and refreshed by the night's uninterrupted sleep, he left the studio.

Yesterday he was on a mission to find his former conspirators. Today he only wanted to participate in life on the streets, enjoy the sounds, the smells, and excitement of the beginning of a new day. Piero needed this street panorama to return him to the life he once knew. And it did.

He walked and walked, for how long he had no idea. As he walked up Via Sistina, Maria surprised him suddenly appearing at his side and said, "Buongiorno Piero. I couldn't find a door marked with an 'X' but kept circling the area hoping to find you and, at last, have."

"I'm sorry, I fell asleep when I returned to the studio yesterday and never cut the mark into the door. Let me take you there."

They continued up the street and he pointed to the door. They kept walking and she said, "I talked to Donatangelo. He wants to see you as soon as possible. No need to wait for the next meeting of the group. Can you come now?"

"Yes, I can."

"We're not returning to where we met yesterday. We're going to Trastevere," said Maria as she turned back toward the Piazza Barberini. "I'll lead the way. You follow a short distance behind. It's better if we're not seen together."

Maria set a fast pace as she led him through side streets he never knew existed. After they crossed the Tiber River she headed directly to the Piazza Santa Maria in Trastevere, and from there a short distance to a small workshop open to the street.

He followed her into the workshop where three men were carving cameos. She walked past them to a small room in the back. Piero hesitated, but one of the carvers signaled for him to follow her. She waited, then led him past stacked amphorae in the back of the room and down steps into a cellar. There, he could make out his old friend Donatangelo behind a candle-lit table covered with papers, he jumped to his feet and welcomed Piero with a warm embrace. Maria turned and left.

In the deep authoritative voice Piero remembered he said, "Welcome back to our world". A large man and natural leader who never lacked confidence, Donatangelo continued, "We were all concerned for you, but I knew you were too tough to be broken by Gregory's jailers. Maria told me you have a place to stay. Is it suitable?"

"Yes, it is. I'd like to stay with my American friend until I have money for a studio, or at least a space where I can begin to work. It reminds me of my studio before I was imprisoned. I feel comfortable there."

"I understand. She also told me you wanted to begin coming to our meetings. That's good news. A great deal is happening and fast.

We need all the people we can to take advantage of this opening Pio Nono is providing."

"What do you mean by 'opening'?"

"Pio Nono is different from Gregory," Donatangelo explained. "Oppression does not appear to be on his agenda. His reign is only beginning, but if the release of the prisoners is any indication of his attitude we're in for a transformed Papal State. The conspiring revolutionary I am, can only see this as either the decision of an inexperienced naïve leader or a clever move by a diabolical ruler purposely misleading us.

"If it's the latter, we have no idea what to expect. However, I feel strongly it's the former. One would have to be foolish to believe prisoners who previously plotted to overthrow the pope and the government they detested, when set free, would now embrace it."

"I agree. After a year in prison, I can only wish the worst for a government that deprived me of so much."

"Exactly, and there are hundreds more like you who feel the same. It's an excellent opportunity for Young Italy to become more active. I'm waiting to hear from Mazzini, who I'm certain, taken by surprise as we were by this prisoner release, will have much to say," said Donatangelo. "By the way, our group meets next week I should have received new ideas for action from him. In the meantime, do you need money? Let me give you some."

Donatangelo reached under the table for a purse, took out some coins, and handed them to Piero who thanked him and said, "I can't wait until our next meeting. *Ciao*, Donatangelo." He turned and left.

On his walk back to Charles's studio Piero felt a new burst of energy. It seemed like old times. Purpose and direction had returned to his life.

"You were gone a long time," said Charles looking up from his carving when Piero returned to the studio.

"I was up at sunrise and you were sleeping. I went for a walk and when people began to fill the streets, looked for my old friends," said Piero.

"Any luck finding any?"

"No, I found no one."

"Remember we talked about visiting Caffé Greco tonight. Do you still want to go?"

"Yes, I'm much better and that's where I'll probably find my friends. I think I'll lie down for a while. All that walking tired me."

Charles returned to his carving, but it was hard for him to believe Pero had not found any of his friends. This was the second time he'd been walking the streets of Rome with no success. He remembered all the times he left alone and returned late before he went to prison. What Piero did was his business. Better he stayed out of it. Right now, he couldn't be happier with the progress on his commission.

When they arrived at the Caffé Greco Charles looked for his friends and saw many new faces. Piero smiled broadly and left him to join a group unfamiliar to Charles. Clearly, he found his friends. Charles saw his own group and joined them.

"Welcome Charles," said Brown. "Where's your friend Piero? I'm anxious to meet him."

"He's over there," said Charles pointing to him. "I expect he'll join us after he has said hello to his friends. Don't forget it's been a year since they've seen each other and I get the definite impression many in that group, particularly the thin ones, were also released from prison."

"We were commenting on the new faces scattered throughout the café tonight. I agree. I think we're witnessing a reunion of conspirators," said Smyth.

James Winton who had joined the group for the evening said, "You're probably right."

"Winton brought me up-to-date on Mazzini, the man you said your friend mentioned. We're visitors in a city of unrest, and a land possibly on the verge of revolution. I think we all sensed the underlying turmoil during the rule of Gregory, but James told me it goes deeper," said Brown.

Charles noticed Piero approaching the table and rose to introduce him to his American friends. Brown offered him a glass of wine, which he gladly accepted while pulling up a chair to join them. Before he had enough time to swallow his first sip of wine Brown began, "Welcome back. Charles told us you were one of the released prisoners. Congratulations are in order."

Piero's sharp reply surprised everyone. "I'm afraid I can't accept any congratulations. I neither accomplished nor achieved anything the past year. Being a prisoner is only something to forget, not congratulated or celebrated. It's not something I'm proud of."

Embarrassed, Brown replied, "I didn't mean to be discourteous. Please accept my apology."

"I do," said Piero. "After only two days of freedom, prisoner anxiety still lingers. Be patient with me. I shouldn't have replied with such bitterness. It wasn't your doing."

"I understand," said Brown.

After a brief silence Smyth raised his glass and in a boisterous roar yelled, "Let's drink to our new friend Piero. Welcome. Now for some serious drinking."

Hearing the loud toast of Smyth, Piero's friends on the other side of the room also raised their glasses. Soon the two groups merged. The other artists in the café needed little encouragement to join the party and everyone decided to honor the returned heroes.

And drink they did, until the café closed. By then the two groups were the best of friends.

The next morning Charles and Piero were jarred from their drunken sleep by a persistent knocking on the door. Both, suffering from serious morning-after woes, groaned and cursed the unwelcome visitor. Piero assumed it was for Charles, rolled over and covered his ears with his hands. Charles rose slowly and struggled to put on his trousers. His head ached and his mouth was as dry as he could remember. The knocking continued and became louder. Stumbling toward the door he mumbled, "*Momento, momento.*"

He couldn't have been more surprised when he opened the door. The unwelcome guest was a beautiful young woman who, seeing Charles, did her best to suppress a laugh. Standing before this beauty without his shirt, and looking the personification of a hungover drunk, he had never felt so humiliated. He was speechless. She broke the silence with, "Is Piero Cifaldi here?"

"Yes, yes, I'll get him, please come in," said Charles, hurrying back to wake Piero.

He shook him and told him he had a visitor. An angry Piero reluctantly sat up and told him, "It must be a mistake. I've told no one where I'm staying."

"This young woman is asking for you. She obviously knew where you were," replied Charles.

Scrambling to his feet, Piero said, "I'll be right out," and walked to the water basin and began throwing water on his face.

Charles quickly put on a clean shirt, patted down his wrinkled pants, and joined Piero at the water basin. After combing his hair, he returned to the studio. He had only a glance of the beautiful woman before, but that brief glance fascinated him. He needed to have another look. Her thick black hair, brown eyes, and dark Mediterranean skin all came together in an enchanting combination. He needed to find out more about this young beauty and why she was looking for Piero.

When Piero came out of the back-room Charles watched with interest as he gave her a quizzical look, and not necessarily like a lover, which did not go unnoticed by Charles. The possibility these two belonged to the secret society Young Italy bothered him. It would be unusual for a woman to be part of a revolutionary group, but she was looking for Piero and everything he did became more suspicious every day.

"*Buongiorno* Maria. Allow me introduce my American friend, Charles Grimes," said Piero.

"My pleasure," said Maria with a slight bow to Charles, then immediately returning her attention back to Piero.

"Please excuse us," said Piero. "I may be gone for a while." He opened the door and they left.

Charles watched from the doorway as they headed for the Piazza Barberini. At least now he knew her name. No question he was smitten by her beauty, but would he ever see her again?

"Why did you have to come to the studio?" asked Piero as they walked down Via Sistina. "We were going to see each other next week at the meeting."

"Donatangelo wanted to see you today.".

"Why?"

"I don't know. I'll leave you now. Go to his workshop in Trastevere," said Maria, who left him and headed in the opposite direction.

What a bad time to be in a hurry, to do anything, thought Piero. His head hurt and he needed a cup of coffee as soon as possible. Anything to make him feel human again. After stopping for an espresso his head began to clear.

He found Donatangelo in the cellar working at his table. "*Buongiorno* Piero," said Donatangelo. "Thank you for coming so soon."

"How can I help you? Maria told me nothing."

"I need a small favor. A delivery of money for Young Italy will be made tomorrow. For reasons of safety I've tried to use different couriers, but the person scheduled for tomorrow's pickup is sick, seriously ill, and I thought of you. Would you be able to do this?"

"If you think I can, yes."

"Good. This is the way it works. Mazzini sends the money from Milan. There is an extensive network for transporting it from Milan to Rome. Almost all the money is smuggled by farmers taking their produce to the markets in different cities. Several farmer members of Young Italy come to Rome every day. They arrive late in the evening so they can be in place when the merchants come to make their purchases at dawn. They use different markets throughout the city. Tomorrow the delivery will be at the market next to Trajan's ancient market."

"Do I pick up the money during the night or at dawn?"

"You'll meet the farmer at dawn when all the buying and selling takes place. Tomorrow, a farmer will be selling melons on the west side of the market. In case there are other farmers selling melons, he'll be the one wearing a blue bandana."

"How will he recognize me?"

Reaching behind his chair for something Donataangelo said, "Take this blue bandana and wear it. Here's enough money to buy three melons. Remember, three. The blue bandannas and purchase of the three melons should be enough for you to identify each other."

"Will the money be in the melons?

Donatangelo gave a hearty laugh and said, "No, we're not that clever. The farmer will put the money in your bag with the melons. Do you have a bag to use?"

"Thought I'd ask," chuckled Piero. "No, but I did notice my friend Charles has one. I think he'd let me use it. Mind if I ask why me and where this money comes from?"

"I chose you because I trust you. You were a good worker before you were imprisoned. I've had one courier disappear with a shipment of money. We're all poor. It can be tempting. I don't know the source of the money. Mazzini raises it. He has supporters in England and I know there are some noble families in Italy who support our cause. I'll see you tomorrow about noon." Said Donatangelo. "*Buona fortuna.*"

As soon as Piero walked into the studio Charles said, "Who's the girl?"

Taken aback by Charles's aggressiveness Piero answered, "You didn't even ask me where I'd been,"

"You wouldn't have told me anyway. Who's the girl?"

"Up until now you've only focused on completing your commission. Suddenly you ask about a girl. Interesting."

"Is she your lover?"

"Ah, jealousy enters," teased Piero. "I've never seen you like this."

"Stop playing with me. Who's the girl?" demanded Charles.

"Her name is Maria, and she's only a friend. I knew her for a short time before I went to prison."

"Where's she from?"

"All I know is she comes from the mountains of central Italy. I recognize the dialect so I suspect she's from a village near mine. I know no more about her," said Piero.

Charles considered what Piero had said. She found Piero, even though he only had been out of prison for a few days. They left together without hesitation and she seemed to be in a hurry. He might be naïve, but this all pointed to their having worked together in the past, and the obvious conclusion was they were members of a secret group. He decided not to confront him about it. That would only make his friend uncomfortable, perhaps put him on the defensive.

His tone, now conciliatory, Charles said, "Young women rarely knock on the doors of strange men. It puzzled me. What else do you know about her?"

"I'm surprised at how interested you are. I've only had brief contacts with her. She's a laundress and I doubt she has a lover. Like you, I think she's beautiful, but I know this kind of Italian woman. There's more to her than meets the eye. She's strong-willed and I suggest you stay out of her way when she decides to do something. Be careful," said Piero.

"I appreciate the warning, but I'd still like to meet her again. Think you can arrange it?" asked Charles.

"Probably, but let me think about it. She's a complicated woman."

Still tired from the night before and not wanting to oversleep, Piero went to bed at sunset. He woke before dawn and tried not to disturb Charles as he left. Trajan's Market wasn't far and if he got there early he could deliver the money to Donatangelo before noon.

The amount of activity on the streets before dawn surprised Piero who never began his days this early. The aroma of baking bread filled the streets, and fresh loaves were already being delivered.

Farmer's carts surrounded the perimeter of the market. Buying and selling had already begun. Piero entered from the east side and paused to take in the lively scene of commerce. The shouts of farmers extolling the virtues of their fresh produce had a rhythm reminiscent of an opera recitativo. Vigorous hand gestures, accentuating the shouts of both the farmers and merchants haggling over prices, completed the operatic scene.

Piero began to work his way to the west side of the market careful to stay out of the way of overzealous bargaining adversaries. He had no trouble finding the melon farmer wearing a blue bandana. When he approached his cart of melons, the farmer gave him a silent look of recognition. He treated him the same as he did any other customer, beginning a charade of bargaining that confused and amused Piero.

Playing the game as best he could, when they had agreed on a price, Piero handed his bag to the farmer who filled it behind the stack of melons, partially out of Piero's sight. He paid and the farmer handed him back his bag, turned away, and began looking for the next customer, Piero's cue to move on.

He headed for the nearest trattoria and ordered an espresso. It might be too early to find Donatangelo at the cameo workshop.

Standing at the bar, enjoying his morning coffee he wondered how the money would be used. He decided it was premature to ask. Better he waited until they knew him better, and he them.

When he arrived at the cameo shop he found Donatangelo waiting for him at his table, who welcomed him by asking if he had any difficulty at the market.

"No," said Piero, handing him the bag. Donatangelo reached in and removed the melons and a small package. When he unwrapped it, what Piero saw made his jaw drop. It was stack of neatly-tied bank notes. He had never seen so much money before.

Donatangelo smiled, "Now we have money to purchase guns and ammunition. It's not enough for everything we need, but it's a start. Piero, I watched you at our meetings and admired the work you did for Young Italy before you were put in prison. I've spoken to former prisoners from your cell and they all agreed, you never wavered from your loyalty to Young Italy.

"I know I can trust you. I wonder if you'd be interested in working with me to purchase arms for Young Italy? It could be dangerous, but after what you've been through, I know you can do it. Think about it and we can talk more after the meeting next week."

Piero now realized this morning's operation had been a test and he had passed. He didn't need any more time to consider the proposal and answered, "I'd like to give it a try."

"See you at the meeting," said Donatangelo. "Here, take one of the melons with you and give the other two to the men in the workshop upstairs."

Piero spent the following days before the Young Italy meeting working on a clay figure. Clumsy at first, his past skills, once intuitive, gradually reawakened. It felt good. The private creative world he inhabited as he worked, helped to blunt the anguish and resentment that haunted him.

The day before the Young Italy meeting Maria stopped him in the street to let him know where it would be held. Before she could turn around and disappear into crowd. he grabbed her by the arm and said, "You have an admirer. My American friend Charles wants to see you."

"I noticed how he looked at me. It's flattering, and he's handsome, but you know we must be careful not to let strangers become too close. You never know when you may be dealing with a spy."

"I can assure you he's not a spy. He only thinks of his work. He's a good friend who has given me a place to stay and recuperate."

Maria pulled her arm from his grasp and turning away, said abruptly, "See you tomorrow."

There were hugs of joy as Piero entered the meeting room the next day. Donatangelo opened the meeting with, "First, let's not forget our four comrades who have not retuned. This injustice to those who struggled beside us must never be forgotten. Everything we do will be not only to further the movement to unite Italy, but also to avenge their deaths and the deaths of all the others resulting from the brutality of Pope Gregory." All nodded in agreement and shouts of, "*Viva Italia*" filled the room.

Donatangelo waited until they were silent., "Communications from Mazzini have been nonstop since Pio Nono became pope. A new enthusiasm and sense of urgency permeates all his writing."

"What do you mean by urgency?" asked one of the men.

"He sees this major shift in policy of Pio Nono as an opportunity. His release of prisoners indicates a tolerant and liberal leader, one who should be tested," said Donatangelo.

"There certainly has been a surprising change in Vatican attitude," said another man in the group. "Don't you think it too early to challenge Pio Nono's leadership? After all, his action of releasing of the prisoners was welcomed by all. To respond with provocation so soon might stop any further reform. Don't forget, Pio Nono must not only deal with us, he has a Curia of shrewd conservative cardinals to work with who have all been selected by and in the mold of Gregory. I doubt they'll welcome any change. It may be a time for patience."

"You're right," said Donatangelo. "I think we all have considered the problem of the cardinals, and it would be hard for me to believe Mazzini hasn't. He feels it's time to move. This first indication of a liberal course by Pio Nono is a time to challenge his authority. Gregory dealt swiftly and firmly with any challenge to his authority. Now we must determine how Pio Nono will react to any opposition."

"Are we prepared to do this?" asked Piero.

"That's the purpose of this meeting," said Donatangelo. "Mazzini has asked me to direct the campaign in Rome. I've met with the leaders of other groups of Young Italy in Rome, and they have agreed to follow our lead. I'll meet with them periodically to plan our strategy of dissent. Once we have a plan, you'll work with members of the other groups to train them in how to best make their voices heard throughout the city."

"What about the press?" asked one of the others. "It's still controlled by the Vatican?"

"There has been no indication from Pio Nono whether he'll continue the strict control over the press," said Donatangelo. "If he removes the current controls over the press, it'll be a definite sign of a liberal direction to his rule and that will be the time to further accelerate our activities. This is an exciting time for Young Italy."

A chorus of "*si, si*" filled the room causing Donatangelo to pause before he continued. "We must continue to operate in secrecy, but don't hesitate to recruit any new members you feel can be trusted and helpful to Young Italy. We'll meet every other week. By the next meeting I should have a final plan of action approved by all the group leaders we can send to Mazzini for his comments and approval."

CHAPTER THREE

The Pope's Carriage

C harles's work was progressing well, and after the first month of carving the rough outline of his sculpture became clear. At this rate he would be finished in another two months. He wanted to see Maria again, but the elusive Piero was never around long enough to convince him to arrange it.

One morning he needed a break from carving and walked to his favorite trattoria. Neighborhood patrons lined the bar and Charles ordered a coffee. As the waiter set a cup of espresso on the bar before him, he said, "Are you going to see Pio Nono this morning?"

Surprised by the question Charles replied, "No, why do you ask?"

"Everyone's going. It's always a good show."

"Is he coming down this street?"

"No, but close by. Pio Nono will be leaving the Quirinal for St. Peter's Basilica and usually passes on Via del Tritone, only a short distance from here," said the waiter.

Charles decided it would be an interesting way to spend a morning. Like a true Roman he downed his espresso in one gulp and headed for the Via del Tritone. He had never seen Pope Gregory and this was his chance to see his first pope.

When he arrived at Via del Tritone people were lining both sides of the street. It reminded him of the people of Washington waiting for the beginning of the Fourth of July parade. Curious about how the people felt about Pio Nono, he walked along the edge of the crowd listening to the nonstop chatter. People in the crowd spoke of Pio Nono lovingly. Charles heard no one making negative comments.

Growing up in Washington he'd seen the president walking on the wood sidewalks near the Capitol, but there were no crowds lining the muddy streets, only a few of his friends from Congress walking with him.

What a difference between Italy and America. Power manifested in completely different ways in two cultures. Pio Nono was not only the Pope who had ecclesiastical authority over the spiritual lives of his subjects, but was also King of the Papal States giving him absolute power to make all the decisions affecting their lives.

Charles recalled the spontaneous political discussions in the taverns at home. They could become heated and passionate and never hesitated to openly criticize the political party in power or the president. No one in America believed political power was absolute. In the end, they always reverted to the Constitution and its guarantees of freedom.

This was the first time Charles had thought about the American Constitution since leaving home. He wished he had a copy. Did Rome or the Papal States have a Constitution? He had no idea. Perhaps he should take an interest in the political discussions occurring nightly at the Caffé Greco.

He waited for at least an hour in the place where everyone said the Pope's carriage would be turning onto the Via del Tritone from the Quirinal. At last he heard murmurs from the crowd, "He's coming." He moved to the edge of the street and stretched his neck to see what they saw. A wave of cheering advanced down the street toward where he stood. He could see two men on large white horses leading the pope's entourage.

Once he could see beyond the lead horses Pio Nono's carriage came into view. Charles's unexpected reaction surprised him. His heart beat faster and he felt a spontaneous sense of excitement. Four magnificent white horses were pulling an elegant carriage flanked by two Swiss guards walking along each side. The midday sun reflected off their shiny metal helmets, and each was armed with a broadsword.

Four Coachmen, two seated in the front, one driving, and two standing on the back with their hands resting on the roof completed Pio Nono's escort. The ornate carvings on the body of the carriage and the wheel's spokes were covered with gold leaf.

In the center of the side door was the gold coat of arms of Pio Nono. The window of the center door was open, but the two side windows were covered with maroon velvet drapes partially obscuring the view of the pope. Charles watched as the white-gloved right hand with the oversized papal ring darted in and out from behind the drapes, bestowing his blessing on the crowd. Almost everyone in the crowd made the sign of the cross, some bowed, and many shouted "*Viva Papa, Viva Papa.*"

Enthralled by the pageantry and elegance of the moment, Charles was startled when a woman bolted from the crowd, ran past the two Swiss Guards, and tossed what looked like a large envelope through the open window of the carriage. Completely caught off guard, the Swiss Guards never had a chance to seize her.

Chaos erupted. Women screamed and people scattered in every direction fearing it might be a bomb. Before pursuing the fleeing woman, the Swiss Guards rushed to see if the pope had been injured. Then Charles realized he recognized the woman—it was Maria. He instinctively ran after her as she headed north to the nearest side street.

As soon as she entered the street a man led his donkey cart across the entrance to the street, almost blocking Charles, who continued after the swift Maria. He could hear the Swiss Guards behind him slowed by the donkey cart, shouting for someone to stop her. No one volunteered.

She turned right, into another narrow street, with Charles behind and gaining ground. The Swiss guards sounded as though they were closing in on them both, when Charles noticed she was heading for Via Sistina. He caught up to her as she reached it, grabbed her by the arm and pulled her a short distance down the street as she struggled to free herself. He unlocked his studio door, and practically threw her in before slamming it shut.

Maria pulled a knife from beneath her skirt ready to defend herself, but as she looked around a puzzled look came over her face and she lowered the knife and said, "You're Piero's American friend, aren't you? Now I recognize where I am."

"Yes. Put the knife away. I'll not harm you, you're safe here."

"Why have you done this? This is none of your business and you may be caught or will be in trouble if the police discover you hid me."

"I wanted to be certain you were safe. That was a bold and brave act. What did you toss into the Pope's carriage? It looked like an envelope, not a bomb. It happened so fast I couldn't tell."

She smiled. "No, not a bomb, but yes, an envelope. That's all I can tell you. This is Roman business and you are an American, so no more questions."

"Are you hurt? I had to be rough with you to convince you to follow me."

"You're strong and were rough, but fortunately for you, surprised me. I couldn't reach my knife. If I had, I might have stabbed you. I didn't recognize you."

"The man with the donkey cart, was he part of the plan? He almost blocked me."

"Yes, he was there to slow the Swiss Guards and give me time to get away. We had an escape plan, but you changed all that."

"Sorry. When I saw it was you, I acted out of instinct."

"But we only met once, here. You hardly know me," said Maria.

"True, but I hope now we'll know each other better. Let me get some wine and bread. You shouldn't go out. They'll still be searching the area," said Charles as he went into the back room.

While he was gone she smoothed down her dress and tried to straighten her hair. Why had this American risked so much to help her? Men, at least the one's she knew never treated her with much respect. Her male colleagues in Young Italy considered her a servant or messenger, someone to perform menial tasks, not one to be part of the serious work of the secret society.

In the meantime, Charles rushed around the back room picking up the scattered dirty clothes of two men and putting them out of sight as best he could. He returned to the main studio and said, "It would be better if we sat in the back room. Please come, I have the wine and bread on the table. I'm afraid it's all I can offer you."

"Thank you, it'll be fine. For an American, you speak good Italian."

"I've been here for over a year now and Italian, for some unknown reason, came easily to me."

"You and Piero are sculptors. The only sculptures I saw before I came to Rome were of the Blessed Virgin and crucified Christ in our village church. All these sculptures, everywhere you walk in Rome confused me when I first came to the city. Now I'm getting used to them, but don't ask me who they are. I have no idea."

"Perhaps I can give you a sculpture tour sometime".

"Perhaps," said Maria with a coy glance at Charles as she sipped her wine. "Where's Piero and when do you expect him back?"

"I never know when to expect him," said Charles. "Don't worry, you'll be safe here until dark. Then I can accompany you home."

They chatted for the next several hours, Maria wanting to know all about this country 'America'. Charles was more than happy to tell her about his life there and how different it was from Rome. Late in the afternoon they heard the door tof the studio open. Both jumped up, but Charles motioned for her not to move. Then both relaxed when they heard a familiar voice asking, "Charles, are you here?"

"Yes, I'm here," answered Charles who went to greet Piero in the studio.

"I bought pasta for dinner. I'm hungry. Start a fire and put some water on."

"Do you have enough for three?"

"Three? Who else is here?" asked Piero. And, as if on cue, Maria walked into the studio, much to Piero's surprise. He looked as though he had seen a ghost. "Maria, what are you doing here? We've been looking for you all day. You know where you were supposed to have gone. We thought you were captured."

"Charles changed my plans," said Maria. "I was on my way to meet you when he grabbed me and hid me here."

"I'm sorry," said Charles. "I was watching Pio Nono's procession and after she tossed the envelop into his carriage and fled, I thought the Swiss Guards would catch her. I ran after her, caught her, and pushed her into the studio. I had no idea you were waiting to help her. It's all my fault."

"At least you're safe," said Piero. "You can tell me all about it later."

Charles interpreted that to mean there will be no further discussion about why Maria ended up in the studio. He understood and volunteered, "Let's get busy and make the pasta. We can make *alio e olio* pasta." From that point on Piero dominated the conversation, never mentioning the incident with Pio Nono's carriage. At sundown, Piero insisted on taking Maria home alone, telling Charles he would save him the walk.

Walking out the door Maria said, "*Ciao*," put her hand on Charles's arm and looked into his eyes with the same coy expression he had seen from her when he suggested he take her on a tour of the sculptures of Rome.

Alone in the studio he sat down to reflect on everything that had happened on this eventful day. The past year had been devoted to studying sculpture with a master. The demands of Professor Moretti and little money to spend beyond the basics for food and shelter had kept him in a restricted world of marble and men.

Twice, Charles had joined his fellow students and artists from the Caffé Greco after a night of drunken carousing for a visit to a bordello. Those nights had cost him dearly. He couldn't afford such extravagance on his meager budget. Those were his last encounters alone with a woman, and he had no idea of how to court a respectable woman. No question he was smitten, but was Maria? He hoped so.

Piero did not return until long after he went to bed and slept late the next morning. By then, Charles had already worked for several hours. The steady pounding of the chisel on marble never disturbed Piero. He slept soundly when Charles carved. He concluded the steady rhythm of the hammer and chisel worked as good as any sleep potion he might buy at a *farmacia*.

"*Buongiorno*, Charles. You certainly surprised me yesterday," said Piero as he entered the studio late in the morning. "You told me you wanted to meet Maria, and I would have introduced you. Kidnapping wasn't necessary." Both laughed.

"I never expected to meet her that way. It was a spontaneous reaction. I had no idea I could do that. But, I'd do it again."

"Let's hope it doesn't happen again. Someone could get hurt. No question you like this woman, but I warned you she can be like a tigress protecting her cubs when challenged. But some men like strong women," said Piero.

"I'm going to do my best to see her again. Where does she live?"

Piero hesitated, turned, and began to walk away without answering, but then at the door of the studio, looked back over his shoulder, and gave Charles an address. "You're on your own, my friend. "*Buona fortuna*," he said as he walked out the door.

Not sure if he should have given him Maria's address, Piero went directly to Trastevere to tell Donatangelo what had happened to her. After hearing the story Donatangelo thought about it for a while, then said, "Let them be. Police will be unlikely to stop and question a woman with an American. Your friend, need not know that his new love is our best messenger for Young Italy."

It took two days before the incident with the pope's carriage appeared in the newspaper. By then all Rome already knew. The article described the sudden rush to the carriage by an unknown woman and her flight, but gave no further information concerning what the mysterious woman had tossed into the carriage.

Charles had little doubt Young Italy planned the incident. If he knew what the envelope contained it could be the evidence he needed to confirm his suspicions and decided to visit Caffe Greco.

He found, Brown, Smyth, and Winton there enjoying the camaraderie and wine defining the ambience of the café. As soon as he sat down Smyth said, "We don't see you often enough. You must be finished with your commission?"

"Hardly, but it's moving along on schedule," said Charles.

You've missed some good times," said Brown. "The mood in here has been elevated to previously unheard-of heights by the actions, or, if you prefer, inactions, of Pio Nono."

"Yes, I do hear a lot about Pio Nono on the streets. That incident with his carriage, what was that all about?" asked Charles.

"I'm surprised you even heard about it," said Winton.

"I saw an article in the paper," said Charles. "It seemed curious. Do you know anything about it?"

"More than curious. A friend at the English Embassy told me that the envelope contained a letter to Pio Nono," said Winton.

"Don't keep us in suspense. What did it say. and who sent it? I'm betting on Mazzini."

"You're right, they say Mazzini wrote Pio Nono asking him to become active in the fight against the Austrians in the north and to lead the fight for unification of Italy. He wants him to begin by sending troops to Ferrara," said Winton.

"Why Ferrara?" asked Brown.

"The Austrians have moved troops there and are threatening the stability of the region," said Winton. "Pope Gregory would never challenge the presence of the Austrians. It will be interesting to see if Pio Nono responds to these two provocations; the one by Austria, and the other by Mazzini. If he does, we'll know he truly wishes to become a leader of all Italy."

"What do you think will happen?" asked Smyth.

"Hard to tell," replied Winton, "but I doubt Young Italy will cease their drive for unification."

"This is becoming interesting. I hear more and more about the secret societies in Rome. Does anyone know someone active in one of the societies?" asked Brown.

All, including Charles, shook their heads, no. He could never say anything that would put Piero or Maria in danger. The evening at Caffé Greco had, however, given him the information he wanted. For the next few days Charles's carving became erratic, with brief periods when he could do no wrong, interspersed with longer periods during which he had poor control of his chisel and made no progress. Thinking of Maria occupied all his waking moments, making it impossible for him to concentrate. He had to meet her again.

Resolving the problem came sooner than Charles anticipated. Donatangelo had received a shipment of pamphlets from Mazzini for distribution to all the Young Italy groups in Rome. They were important and outlinied detailed instructions for organizing demonstrations to critisize Pio Nono's lack of leadership.

Interception of these pamphlets by the police would undo all the work he and the other groups of Young Italy had done to prepare for this campaign. Donatangelo immediately thought of his most dependable messenger, Maria. He knew she could do it, but not alone, and needed an assistant. He liked his idea that the police would be unlikely to stop an Italian woman accompanied by an American. Piero said the American was infatuated with Maria and assured Donatangelo he could be trusted.

At first, she balked when they explained their plan. She liked the American but thought he might be too naïve and untested in the complicated world of Roman politics. The stakes were high, and she would never forgive herself if anything went wrong. She insisted she could do it alone. But they persisted and convinced her the plan would work. After all, Charles didn't need to know what they were distributing. His presence would give an innocent appearance to their passage through the streets of Rome.

The next morning Piero woke earlier than usual, complaining he felt sick. He wondered if Charles would do him a favor. He had promised to help Maria make some deliveries. Would he help her? Charles, of course jumped at the opportunity.

Maria lived a ten-minute walk from the studio. He couldn't get there fast enough and found her outside her building talking with a small group of neighborhood women. He hesitated to interrupt their lively conversation, but finally found the courage to approach them. Still unsure of himself said, "Sorry to interrupt you Maria, but may I talk to you?"

The women ceased talking and scrutinized this handsome young man with a foreign accent. She had never before given any indication she had any male friends. They often teased her about it and were now hoping to find out who this was. Seeing how curious all her friends were Maria replied quickly, "Of course. Please excuse us." All eyes were on the two as they walked away. When they were far enough away not to be heard, Maria stopped and asked what she already knew, "What brings you here?"

"Piero is sick and said he had promised to help you today," said Charles. "He asked if I would help you instead. Is that all right with you?"

Pressing on with Donatangelo's plan she asked, "Will he get better or should I go to help him?"

Momentarily flustered and concerned his visit with Maria was about to end prematurely, he said, "No, no, he should be better by tomorrow. He told me you had deliveries to make today."

"Yes, it'll take time, possibly all day. Can you be away from the studio that long

"I can. I'll help you."

"Follow me," said Maria and she began the walk toward Trastevere. She moved fast and Charles had trouble keeping up with her through the morning crowds.

Once across the river, she led him to Donatangelo's cameo workshop. Charles stopped to watch the cameo carvers, while she proceeded to the back room. She returned and then pointed to a wheelbarrow loaded with two trunks and said, "That's what we'll be delivering."

"Luggage. Is someone moving?"

"Yes, and today we're the movers."

He walked to the back of the workshop and lifting the wheelbarrow, found it heavier than expected. The trunks were too heavy to be filled with clothing, but he said nothing and pushed it into the street.

"We'll be making deliveries all over the city. You may regret volunteering to help me."

"Never. I enjoyed the time we had at the studio. You spent all our time listening to my stories. It's time to hear about yours."

Pushing the wheelbarrow on cobblestone streets proved difficult, but he knew it would grow lighter and become easier as the day progressed. Maria led him to the first destination across the Tiber River in the northwest area of the city. They stopped in front of a plain building where she told him to wait outside. Before long she returned with two young men who picked up one of the trunks and took it inside. She told him to continue waiting and guard the wheelbarrow. He had hoped he would be present when they opened the trunk to see what it contained.

At the next stop she didn't return immediately. As he waited alone, two policemen came around the corner and were headed toward him. Blinded by his desire spend time with Maria, he never considered the possibility of any danger helping her. He knew the trunks probably contained material being distributed by the secret society. Now, what was he supposed to say if they questioned him?

Close to panic as they approached, and completely inexperienced when it came to dealing with the Roman police, he didn't move from the wheelbarrow. After all, he was an American, a foreigner. He had no idea of the extent of danger he faced.

At the same moment Maria came down the stairs and stopped in the stairwell watching the scene from behind. The policemen asked Charles what he was doing. Without thinking he automatically answered in English, "Moving to another apartment."

When the policemen heard they were dealing with an American they smiled and replied in Italian, "You should get a donkey," and laughing, moved on. When they were out of sight, Maria exited the building and said, "You think fast. I'm impressed."

Basking in the compliment Charles had the good sense to say no more. He also had the good sense to pretend he did not know they were delivering revolutionary material. Near the ancient ruins of the church, Santa Costanza, she suggested it would be a good place to stop to eat and rest before the final two deliveries.

He found a trattoria and purchased bread, wine, and splurged on a small amount of cheese and salami. He pushed the wheelbarrow behind a bush and they settled next to a line of cypress trees to enjoy their lunch.

Maria was touched. No man had ever treated her so generously. Charles said, "I know nothing about you. Tell me about yourself."

"It wouldn't interest you. You've traveled a long distance to Rome and know about the world. I'm a peasant girl who was never far from my mountain village before I came to Rome. I could tell listening to you in your studio you come from a loving home, a home to which you'll eventually return. I'm afraid I've been cursed to live my life alone. I've been in Rome for two years and don't know where I might be from month to month."

Maria paused and sighed. "I'm realistic about my future and want to be honest with you. No one has shown the interest in me you have and I'm grateful, but you have a bright future before you as an artist. You don't need the trouble I can bring to your life, a privileged life."

He interrupted, "Are you an orphan? Why do you say you're cursed?"

"You're the first person to whom I'll answer that question. I came to this city from a small village in the mountains south of Rome. Sixteen and alone, the first year I almost starved to death, but never gave up and learned how to survive on the streets."

Confused, Charles asked, "Why can't you return home?"

"My father will never allow it."

"What do you mean never? That's cruel."

"It's cruel, but a reality of the life of peasants and their families. What the father says, right or wrong, proven or unproven, is the law. He listened to village gossip and determined I had been *familiare* with a boy. He was wrong, but as far as he was concerned, his and the family's honor had been disgraced. It made no difference that he was wrong. The mere suggestion I had disgraced the family ended my life in my home and village."

"You'll never go back?"

"Never. This struggle has changed me. As poor and alone as I am, I've developed a sense of pride and achievement. It's hard to explain, particularly to a man. Can I love someone after all this or can they love me? I'm not sure. That's why I'm telling you all this now."

"But you've said I interest you. I'll take that to mean you'd be willing to see me again. Am I right?"

"Yes, but I don't wish to hurt you, or put you in danger," said Maria.

"I'm not a Roman, but after watching the activity of you and Piero, I have an idea of who you two work for. I think I know what was in the envelope you tossed into Pio Nono's carriage and have a good idea of what we're doing today. In no way does that change how I feel about you. Understand?" said Charles with all the sincerity he could muster.

Maria didn't reply and looked down as though deep in thought. After a long pause, she reached out, and briefly covered his hand with hers. They finished their meal in silence. She never confirmed his suspicions, only saying, "It's time for us to move on."

The remaining deliveries proceeded without incident and they finished in the southwest quadrant of the city, across the Tiber River from Trastevere. When they returned the wheelbarrow to the cameo workshop, Maria asked him to wait for her. She walked to the back of the shop and disappeared behind the stacked amphorae. He was tempted to follow her but knew he was not welcome in that part of her secret world. She returned quickly.

Now, early evening, they joined the crowds of Romans in the streets enjoying their *passegiata*, or evening stroll. Convinced the wheelbarrow had bounced over every cobblestone in the streets of Rome, his back ached. She could tell from the way he walked he was in pain and said," Let's stop at my favorite place to relax and watch the sunset." This unexpected invitation pleasantly surprised Charles.

She led him to the Roman Forum and there headed toward the tall columns in the center. "Those are the ruins of the Temple of Saturn," said Charles.

"Now I know the name of one ruin. I only come here to relax, not sight-see." The tall columns sat on a broad base of bricks covered with dirt and grass about three meters high. She led him to a crude set of stairs formed by the crumbling bricks. "Follow my footsteps. This is my secret path, but be careful, some of the bricks are loose."

At the top, she pointed to where he should sit and said, "You can lean against the column, rest your back, and watch the sunset from here."

"The view of the Forum from up here is special," said Charles. "It accentuates the outlines of the collapsed buildings better than when you're walking through the ruins. A perfect place to sit and imagine how Rome looked in its glory."

"And a perfect place to escape," said Maria.

The crisp cool air of early fall and the changing patterns of light and shadow on the surrounding ruins created a magical scene. And at this time of day, everything was underscored by the peace and quiet within the Forum. After about twenty minutes, Charles knew what he wanted to do next, but at the same time did not wish to spoil his chances of seeing Maria again by acting aggressively. He remembered Piero had told him to move slowly with Maria.

Less inhibited, Maria took charge of the situation, rolled into his arms and kissed him. Then she jumped up and extended her hand, helping him to his feet. For a brief moment, Charles was surprised, but took her hand, stepped right into her arms, and kissed her passionately.

She did nothing to resist, but when he finally released her she stepped back and took a deep breath, as did he. A Roman man would not have stopped there. In the back streets of the city, she had witnessed numerous struggles and ugly beatings of women who resisted the advances of men. This had left her hesitant to become involved with a man, but now knew she had found one she could love.

"I think we should go before it gets too dark and dangerous here," said Maria.

Charles momentarily panicked hoping he had not insulted her with his aggressive kiss, but she put his anxiety to rest when she calmly took his hand and led him down the steps of her secret path. She didn't release it until they were outside the Forum.

When thy parted at the Piazza Barberini, she took both his hands sand pulled herself up against him and said, "Thank you for your help. What a pleasant day. A day I'll always remember."

Charles, struggling to keep his emotions under control, had the good sense to give her the polite perfunctory kiss on each cheek appropriate for the setting.

"*Ciao*. Will I see you again?".

"I'd like that. I'll contact you one way or another. I think you understand. *Ciao*," said Maria who turned and walked away.

He didn't move until she disappeared into the crowd.

Back at the studio, and unable to sleep, he relived every moment of the day, perhaps the happiest of his life. At least for now it felt that way. Maria liked him and may have even shown him his first glimpse of love. He did not want that feeling to fade.

Something else happened. Risking discovery by the police as they made their deliveries introduced a new feeling of adventure. A feeling absent in the studio. Carving marble was a lonely business and the rewards came ever so slowly. The rewards today, though risky, were immediate and exciting.

CHAPTER FOUR

The Civic Guard

Pio Nono can always depend on one supporter, the wine carrier, Ciceruacchio. I listened to him in the Piazza Navona today, praising his beloved pope. He's a better preacher than any cleric in the Vatican and the large crowds he attracts believe whatever he says," said Piero.

"You mean Angelo Brunetti? Yes, he's Pio Nono's most reliable advocate on the streets," said Donatangelo. "I've heard him speak. Best we avoid any confrontation with him. As you say, he has the ear of the people and you'll only lose if you challenge him. He's not a member of Young Italy and we should keep it that way."

"Pio Nono has done an excellent job of expanding the Civic Guard," said Piero. "He's recruiting and arming these troops as fast as he can. Now with the Swiss Guards, police, and remainder of Gregory's troops he has a significant army at his disposal. We haven't acquired additional arms in the past three months. Do you plan to buy anymore?"

"I want the members of Young Italy to join the Civic Guard. Let Pio Nono arm them," said Donatangelo. "Civic Guards are being expanded in the other provinces. Mazzini thinks they'll be an essential component of the troops we'll need to fight the Austrians when the time comes."

"The other groups agree with this strategy?"

"I'm meeting with all the leaders today."

"Then I suppose I should join the Civic Guard," said Piero.

Piero watched as Charles circled his sculpture making minor, insignificant changes on his commission, and finally said, "When are you going to finish this? You know you can overwork a piece. It looks perfect to me, don't ruin it."

"You're right, I probably should quit. Do you think it's ready?"

"Yes, I meant it. It's good. Time to ship it and move on to something new. Any new prospects?"

"Winton has sent several Americans to the studio. There's one good prospect. They're leaving Rome next week so I should hear something soon. If I ship this now, depending on the weather, it could be in Boston by Christmas."

"Do it. I know it must feel like losing your firstborn, but the time has come.".

"What have you been up to? You continue to be gone every day until late every night," asked Charles not expecting an answer.

"I'm going to surprise you and tell you what I'm about to do."

"This is hard to believe. Let me sit down," said Charles sarcastically.

"I think you should sit down for this one. Today I plan to enlist in Pio Nono's Civic Guard. I'll be protecting Rome. That should make you feel safe."

Charles, looked stunned, "You, the one who has no love whatsoever for the pope. Are you serious?"

"I'm serious."

Charles thought about this. His friend sounded sincere, but he knew he had to interpret what Piero said in light of his involvement with Young Italy. Were they infiltrating the Civic Guard and planning to sabotage it or take it over? Piero would never tell him, but it further proved to him how devious Young Italy operated in their quest for the unification of Italy.

"What will this Civic Guard be used for?"

"To reinforce the army and police of the Papal States. In the north, where the Austrians are threatening Bologna and Ferrara the provinces already have Civic Guards."

"Doesn't this increase Pio Nono's power?"

"I suppose it's hard for an American to understand. I don't think I can explain it to you."

"No need to explain. We understand. In America we called our Civic Guard a militia. Our Revolutionary Army was formed from militias. That's what makes all this interesting to me. Are you going to stay here after joining?"

"The Civic Guard is not a permanent commitment. The troops go on with their lives and serve only as needed when crises arise. You can't get rid of me so easily."

"I think you can understand why it's difficult for me to picture you as a soldier taking orders. You've always resisted authority, but I wish you the best. I can't wait to hear more about this Civic Guard," said Charles. "Promise you'll tell me all about it when you come back."

"I will," said Piero.

"The drinks are on me tonight," announced Charles to his friends at the Caffé Greco.

"This is indeed a special night. Charles is buying," said Smyth. "Why this unexpected treat?"

"Yes, unexpected, but welcome," said Brown. "I accept the offer."

"I'm celebrating the completion of my first commission. Tomorrow they come to crate it for shipping and then it leaves for America."

"Any luck with the two couples I sent to visit your studio?" asked Winton.

"One will be retuning this week. I gave them drawings to review. It looks promising," said Charles.

The wine arrived and all raised their glasses exclaiming in unison, "*Salute!*"

"How's your friend Piero these days?" asked Brown.

"As always, gone most of the time," said Charles. "Seems busy all the time doing what I never know, except for today. For the first time he surprised me and told me his plans. He's joining the Civic Guard."

"Where do they train?" asked Smyth

"I've watched them marching in the Circus Maximus. It looks as if there are different units training every day," said Brown.

"Yes," said Winton. "Because of Pio Nono's popularity, enlistments are up. How they'll perform in battle is another question."

"Are they preparing to join the other Civic Guards in the north?" asked Charles.

"That's the big question. Will Pio Nono allow his army and the Civic Guard to fight the Austrians and their experienced troops?" said Winton. "It's now known the envelope tossed into Pio Nono's carriage contained a message from Mazzini. A message challenging Pio Nono to take the lead in the struggle for the unification of Italy. Mazzini has thrown down the gauntlet. Will Pio Nono pick it up and accept the challenge? That's what everyone's waiting to find out."

Charles ordered more wine. This was a time to celebrate. A work of his would soon arrive in America and Maria liked him. At least he thought so, but it was premature to mention that possibility to his friends

"While watching the Civic Guard train in the Circus Maximus I saw two of our fellow American sculptors marching with the new enlistees. It surprised me. I didn't know they allowed expatriates to join," said Brown. "Winton, were you aware we could join the Civil Guard?"

"I heard rumors that non-Romans were volunteering. Like you I'm surprised, but when you think about it, I'm never surprised by what happens in this city or Italy for that matter," said Winton.

"An adventure," shouted Smyth encouraged by an evening of male camaraderie and wine. "My life story lacks a thrilling adventure. My biographers will only have my beautiful paintings to extoll. Of course, they're good enough to stand on their own, but they'll be even greater in the light of a heroic deed."

Everyone laughed, and Brown added, "Indeed, how can we forget the trials of Caravaggio after he fled the scene of his crime of murder and Michelangelo's memorable quarrels with Pope Julius and participation in the fortifications of Florence. These dramas energized the pens of the foremost biographers for years."

A chorus of, "Hear, hear" came from Charles, Brown, and Winton.

"You jest," said Smyth, "But the more I think about it the more serious I become. Why not? I love this city and need something like this to reinvigorate both myself and my artistic muse."

"You're certain it's not the wine encouraging you?" said Winton.

"No," said Smyth, "I've decided. I'm going to join the Civic Guard. Anyone else interested?"

A somber silence came over the group as everyone looked down into their drinks thinking about what they'd heard. Brown broke the silence and astonished everyone when he said, "Smyth, you're right, I also need to revitalize my artistic muse. I've spent far too much time either in my studio or in libraries, or here. I'll join with you."

After the shock of Brown's announcement abated Smyth said, "How about you Charles and James?"

Winton did not hesitate to answer. "It would be inappropriate for the American consul in Rome to also be a member of the Civic Guard of Rome. As they say, "one cannot serve two masters." As soon as word got back to Washington I'd be asked to step down as the American consul."

Charles listened in silence, giving no hint of what he thought of the drama playing out before him. All he could think about was Maria and her dedication to Young Italy. She believed in a cause and put all at risk to support that belief. Causes had never been a part of his life. The more he thought about it, he had to admit life as an artist could be a sanctuary of self-indulgence. Was he prepared to abandon this sanctuary and be as brave as Maria? Time to find out.

The eyes of the others were all focused on him. Charles rose and pretended to begin walking away from the table, but after one step turned abruptly, and shouted, "Count me in."

They all jumped up and cheered and hugged one another before reaching for their glasses to once again raise them and exclaim in unison, "*Salute!*" Patrons at the surrounding tables looked either puzzled or grinned at the antics of the mad Americans.

The next morning Piero watched Charles as he got out f bed and stumbled toward the water pitcher and emptied it in rapid gulps.

"Looks like you had a good time last night. Are you all right?" asked Piero.

"Not yet. Coffee would be welcome. Would you mind getting me some, please?"

"I will."

When the young boy arrived with the tray holding two cups of espresso he barely made it through the door before Charles grabbed a cup and downed it. He sat a while before he spoke, "Yes, we had a good time last night. We did our best to set a record for wine consumption at Caffé Greco. I have a terrible headache. I like your Italian words for headache – *mal di testa*. You can capitalize *mal*, even underline it, twice."

"I know the feeling. What were you celebrating?"

"It began innocently, celebrating the completion of my commission. Then it turned serious. In considering what happened last night, I wonder if I did the right thing."

"You're having second thoughts about what? Not an unusual consequence after a night like that."

"What you mentioned yesterday, the Civic Guard. Three of us decided to join."

"*Oh Dio*, you and your American friends are going to join the Civic Guard. Why?" asked an astonished Piero.

"Probably three different reasons. It doesn't matter, we're all committed to joining. Tell me what I'm about to do. What is this Civic Guard all about?"

"You're Americans, not Romans, but if you insist, I'll tell you as much as I know having only joined myself yesterday. You must make a commitment for at least six months. They'll give you a uniform and sword and after you complete the first full week of training you'll be training only one day each week. The initial training consists mainly of marching, learning how to take orders, and understanding military discipline. When they decide you're ready they train you to fire a musket."

"What type of duty can you be assigned?"

"From what I've heard, manning the various gates of Rome, patrolling streets. Things like that. If Rome is under siege the Civic Guard will then act as a reinforcement to the army. Think about it: do you Americans want to take that kind of risk? The way things are going in the north, war is a real possibility."

"I doubt any of us will change our minds. Where do we go to enlist?"

"The headquarters is in the Parliament Building," said Piero. "Good luck my friend, I hope you understand the seriousness of this decision. It may seem a romantic challenge, but if fighting erupts, bullets and canon shot does not discriminate between Romans and well-intentioned Americans."

Despite the disagreeable morning, the remainder of the day improved. The American couple who had shown interest in a possible sculpture returned and, satisfied with the drawings finalized their purchase. With the completion of the recent sculpture and the deposit on this one, Charles's financial situation improved dramatically.

New clothes, better furniture—things he could purchase and enjoy without fear of becoming bankrupt were now possible. The first thing he wanted to purchase was a bed. No more sleeping on a straw mattress on the floor. As he considered his good fortune, someone knocked on the door. When he opened it, the day became even better. It was Maria.

"I hope I'm not disturbing you," she said.

"You know you're welcome anytime. Come in, Come, in. But I have nothing to offer you. Or better yet, do you have time to go for a walk, maybe have something to eat?"

"I'd like that."

"Good, we can celebrate another commission together."

"Congratulations Charles. Such good news."

"It's great news, this commission is even larger than the last. I feel like a real sculptor."

"You're not only a real sculptor but a fine one."

"I don't know about that, but I'll accept the compliment. Any encouragement is welcome. Let's take a walk."

"Tell me about this commission. What's it going to be this time?" said Maria.

". They want a life-sized figure of Bacchus."

"Who's Bacchus?"

"He's the god of the grape harvest and associated with wine."

"I don't understand why they would want such a large sculpture. They must have a big house. Or is it for the outside?"

"Yes, they must have a big house and agreed to my price. Much more than my first commission. I'll have to look around to see if I can find any other sculptures of Bacchus."

"You mean they don't know how it'll look? Why would they give you money before they know what they're getting?"

"I made drawings for them. They liked what they saw and now I'll make a clay maquette to use as a guide."

"Will it also be life size?"

"No, the maquette will be about one-third life size."

"But if they're returning to America how will they see it?"

"I'll have a photograph taken and send it to them."

"I've seen these photographs. They're magic but I don't understand how they're done."

"Neither do I, but it's becoming important for my business. Why don't we stop here to eat? I've been here before, the food is good and the price is right," said Charles.

"*Ristorante di Fiori Rosso*" said Maria. "It looks finer than I'm used to."

"This morning I sold another sculpture. I can't think of anyone else I'd rather celebrate this good fortune with than you," said Charles. Maria didn't reply, but Charles didn't miss the slight blush in her cheeks.

When he opened the door, they were greeted by the luscious aroma of a tomato sauce with a hint of garlic. Busy waiters were scurrying back and forth between the tables. They found a table for two and as soon as they sat down a young boy brought them two plates, bread, and an open bottle of wine marked with a crayon at the current level of wine in the bottle. The afternoon's meal and price were written on a chalkboard on the wall next to entrance—*spaghetti con sugo pomodoro*. A simple dish, but the vibrant conversations and satisfied looks on the faces of the patrons said it all. It must be good.

Charles checked the accuracy of the crayon mark on the bottle before pouring the wine, He raised his glass to hers, and said, "*Salute!*" After taking a sip he said, "The wine's not bad. What do you think?"

"I like it. I've become used to the wine of Rome, but when I first came here I didn't. I guess you get used to the wine of your region and all others are strange to your taste. The same with the food, including the bread. I suppose if I went back home the wine and bread there would now taste bad."

"Probably. When I came to Rome I couldn't find anything I liked. Hunger forced me to accept the Roman diet which I now think is tastier than the food I ate in Washington. We never had wine at home. Getting used to the wine of Rome took no time at all," laughed Charles. "At home, we drank milk or water with meals. In the taverns they drank ale and whiskey. Wine is found only in the homes of the wealthy. "And coffee, what a difference. It took time to adjust to espresso."

"Coffee was a luxury in our home. Often, we drank wine instead of water," said Maria. "What's whiskey like?"

"I think whiskey and your grappa would be considered comparable drinks. Both have a high alcohol content. Whiskey is dark, grappa clear."

A waiter arrived with the steaming hot pasta. Both anxious to taste the sauce, took their forks and spoons and began to sample the spaghetti. After a few mouthfuls Maria said, "This sauce is good. Reminds me of home."

Neither spoke as they enjoyed their pasta before it became cold. When Maria finished eating she put her fork and spoon down, sat back, sighed, and said, "I was hungry. Thank you."

"My pleasure."

"Piero told me you and your American friends plan to join the Civic Guard. Is it true?"

"It is."

"Why? You're not Romans. You could get hurt or you could get killed," she said, obviously concerned.

"We live in Rome. We love Rome. Must we always remain strangers?"

"I think they have enough recruits," replied Maria.

"You can never have enough troops."

"So, you think this will be exciting. You have no other reason?"

"I don't know about the other two, but since I met you and discovered what you do, what you believe, I've been thinking," said Charles.

Disconcerted, Maria replied, "How do you know what I believe?"

Leaning closer to her, Charles continued in a whisper, "I know you're dedicated to a cause. Something beyond yourself and your day-to-day life. Let me turn this around and ask, why do you risk your life for this cause?"

That made Maria uneasy and she looked around to see if anyone was close enough to overhear their conversation. Charles looking directly into her eyes continued, "I know you could be arrested for what you do. I'm flattered you're concerned about me. I assure you I'm even more concerned about the danger you face every day".

Maria took her time before responding. "Charles, our lives have been different. I told you of the problem with my father. As far as I know, you've been fortunate to come from a loving home. I've heard of America, the land of equality and hope. When I lived on the streets it didn't take long for me to abandon the possibility of hope. Only survival mattered. I decided I needed to find a way out. Find people who felt the way I did, people, who could change our way of life and perhaps even century's old cruel family customs."

"And you think you have?"

"It's a beginning," said Maria. Then looking around and moving closer to Charles she continued on in a low voice, "Mazzini is focused on unifying Italy, but he does care about people and I can only hope he cares about both men and women. Oh, I shouldn't have mentioned his name."

"Don't worry, I know about him and his crusade to unify Italy," replied Charles.

"I'm uneducated and cannot express myself like Piero or Donatangelo. Do you understand what I'm trying to say?"

"I think I do, but you've only further convinced me I should also become involved in this clash of ideologies and the future of Italy. Maria, never underestimate your intelligence. Your thinking is clear and based on reality. Since I met you I've been thinking and am beginning to recognize my world can be one of self-indulgence and superficialities. You live in the real world."

"I may have said too much. You're the only one to whom I've talked to like this," said Maria.

"Thank you for trusting in me. It means a great deal to me," said Charles. "Let's walk."

As they left the ristorante Maria slipped her arm under his. No woman had ever done that before, but he accepted and appreciated the gesture by pressing her arm tightly against the side of his chest. Arm in arm they joined the other Romans out for a stroll on this late fall afternoon.

They found a bench where they could sit and watch the passing crowd, a first for these two active and ambitious young people completely engrossed in their contradictory worlds. Charles's life in Rome had lacked tenderness and love. Too busy to notice before, life now took a new direction. One he was eager to explore and hoped he would share with her. He wondered if she was thinking the same thing.

After sitting for at least an hour enjoying the passing parade of strollers, the arrival of the cool evening air prompted him to suggest he take her home. They didn't hurry, often stopping to view and discuss the different wares of the street venders. Maria never let go of his arm.

Before they parted she made him promise he would never tell anyone what they had discussed.

***

Two days later Charles convinced Smyth and Brown to go to the Parliament Building and enlist. The enthusiasm exhibited at the Caffè Greco had faded, but nevertheless they agreed.

Because they were Americans they were questioned at length about their reasons for wanting to join the Roman Civic Guard but in the end were accepted. Much to their surprise, they were told they should report to the Circus Maximus for training the next week. Because of the approaching Feast of Christmas they would be the last group of enlistees scheduled until after the New Year.

Smyth and Brown balked at such short notice. Each offered several excuses and Charles had to admit the last-minute notice was inconvenient, but his determination to join the Civic Guard remained firm. He would be there and hoped they would.

When he returned to the studio and told Piero he had joined, he said "I was skeptical you would enlist. I still don't understand. You have nothing to gain. When do you begin training?"

"Next week."

"Next week? I can't believe it. You'll be in the same group I am. Most enlistees have to wait at least a month. You must be important. I didn't know Americans were so highly sought as soldiers," said Piero laughing.

"They know a good deal when they see it. We'll serve together. Amazing."

"Life presents us with so many surprises, but for a change this is a good one. It'll be an honor to serve with you."

"Thanks, I feel the same way," said Charles."

The sun was setting when he left the studio to find Maria. When she saw him he nodded and followed her toward Via Barberini. Once there, he took her by the hand and led her to a quiet corner of a building.

She reacted to the news of his enlistment in the Civic Guard the same way Piero did, but for a different reason. She had hoped, given time, he would forget the idea or they would refuse to enlist Americans. Charles was the first person to enter her life she could love and trust and she did not want to lose him.

"You'll make a good soldier for Rome, but you must promise me you'll be careful and not volunteer for any dangerous duty. I don't want to lose you, my love," said Maria.

This time it was Charles's turn to blush. What she said moved him more than anything ever had. He threw his arms around her and kissed her. Afterward, they both remained silent in each other's arms.

He was the first to speak, "Do you mean what you said?"

"Of course. All I can say is I love you. I knew I loved you the first time I saw you. Is that possible?"

"I hope so. And I love you Maria."

"Let's not say anymore. I want to cherish this moment. Savor it," said Maria.

He reluctantly released her and said, "I'll walk you home now."

Having no idea what to expect on the day they were to report for training, Piero and Charles admitted to nervous stomachs as they walked to the Circus Maximus. Surprisingly, Smyth and Brown were already there as were thirty-six other recruits. After roll call and a short welcoming speech by an officer, two sergeants took charge.

From that moment on these two tall, muscular men with scarred—probably battle-scarred faces—and the loudest voices Charles had ever heard, did nothing but shout a barrage of orders. This went on all morning as the recruits stumbled and staggered attempting to march in order.

For Charles, a result of the verbal abuse of the sergeants was the acquisition of a new colorful repertory of Italian profanity including references to mothers and saints Italians ordinarily considered sacred. He'd never heard anything like it before.

Everyone welcomed the mid-day break and meal. Charles had noticed the heavy breathing of the overweight Smyth as they marched. When they were dismissed he joined him as he lay flat on his back and asked, "Do you think you can continue? You look dog-tired."

"I am," said Smyth. "Do I have any other choice?"

"I guess not."

"I thought we were going to defend Rome, not trample it."

"You'll feel better after you drink some water and get something into your stomach."

"I hope so. Otherwise I don't think I can take six days of this," said Smyth.

Piero and Brown also looked tired, but no more than most of the recruits. The physical demands of the training did not diminish, only increased each day. The three showed no interest in spending their nights at the Caffé Greco after marching all day. Soaking their feet and getting to bed early was their first priority.

They were given uniforms and swords at the end of the fifth day and told to report the next day in uniform. On their last day they at least looked somewhat soldierly and paraded in order, displaying their newfound discipline and pride. At dismissal all the recruits gave a loud, grateful cheer and after saying goodbye to their friends and the new friends they had made, Charles and Piero headed for the studio. They needed a day of rest before resuming their lives.

CHAPTER FIVE

Civitavecchia

Behind schedule, and with the Feast of Christmas approaching, Charles went to Trastevere to purchase a marble block for his new commission. Soon the preparations for Christmas would make passage of a large marble block through the busy streets difficult, if not impossible. The Italians liked to begin celebrating long before a feast as important as Christmas and a good excuse to ignore work.

Piero also went to Trastevere to visit Donatangelo. When he saw him coming down the stairs he said, "Welcome back. I see our new soldier survived his first week of service."

"I survived, but my feet barely made it," said Piero.

"I'm glad you're here. There's something I'd like to discuss with you. I need your help with a request from Mazzini. He met an American journalist in London who was sent by a New York newspaper to write about the political upheavals in Europe. After London, she went to Paris, and after Paris, will end her travels in Rome. He says she's brilliant and writes beautifully. They have become close friends and feels she can help our movement with her dispatches to

New York. We need support and sympathy wherever we can find it and he would like us to give her all the assistance we can while she's here."

"I'm not sure I'm the best choice to assist an American woman in Rome."

"I agree, but I had Maria in mind. You and Maria are good friends. She's one of our most trusted and best workers. Always gets the job done and as far as I'm concerned, the right person for this job."

"I agree. What's the journalist's name and when will she arrive in Rome?"

"Margaret Fuller and she's supposed to reach Rome at the end of March. I wanted your opinion before I talked to her."

"Remember what I told you about Maria. She and my American friend are spending more and more time together."

"That's interesting. Let's not say anything about this to Maria now. She told me her American friend was a big help when the two delivered Mazzini's pamphlets, and said his presence avoided a possible search by the police. The police are hesitant to harass travelers and unlikely to search them. We can talk to her after we get a specific date for the journalist's arrival.

"This brings me to something I'd like you to consider. I asked you before to become involved with the acquisition of arms for Young Italy and you said you were interested. We might not need as many arms as I thought before because of Pio Nono's arming of the Civic Guard," said Donatangelo.

"I think you're right. There are going to be thousands of Civic Guards with muskets in Rome, including me."

"And Mazzini agrees the Civic Guard in the cities will play a major role in the final struggle, but would still like us to use the money he sent for what it was intended, guns and ammunition. Contraband guns are smuggled into Italy from France and Spain at several ports. The closest to us is Civitavecchia."

"Mazzini has given me the name of a man to contact in Civitavecchia who will arrange the purchase of guns. I want you and Maria to find this man, purchase the guns, and make the final arrangements for moving them to Rome. We are supposed to contact this man in five days. Will you do it?"

Piero thought a while before answering, "Why Maria? Can't I do this alone."

"This is a great deal of money. A man and woman traveling to Civitavecchia are less likely to be stopped and searched."

"Do you want me to discuss this with Maria?"

"If you prefer."

"I would," said Piero

"Then we're in agreement. You'll talk to Maria. I'm confident she'll go. We should all meet the day before you leave when I'll give you additional information about the dealer and the money," said Donatangelo.

Piero left Trastevere and went directly to talk to Maria about Donatangelo's proposal.

"What is it this time, Piero?" asked Maria. "Whenever I see you, I can expect a message or assignment from Donatangelo. Am I right?"

"You are. But this one's different. You can't do it alone. We must work together."

"I trust you, Piero, so that should be no problem."

She listened as he explained Donatangelo's plan. When he finished, she asked, "Can we do this in one day? It sounds like we will need more than one day."

"We'll have to stay in Civitavecchia at least one night, perhaps more," he answered. "The longer we stay though, the more likely we could be stopped and searched."

"How do these guns get from Civitavecchia to Rome?"

"I'll take care of the arrangements. I'd like to find this man the first day, complete the purchase of the guns. If I inspect them the next day and transfer the money, we can leave that same day."

"I've never traveled for the group or done anything so different. Why me?"

"He feels as a couple we're less likely to be searched and it's easier to hide money under a woman's dress," said Piero. "Will you do it? Remember, the risk of being stopped around a port is high. And we know nothing about this man who smuggles and sells guns. He' a criminal, but we have no alternative and must deal with him."

"You certainly don't make it sound appealing, but you know me. I'll do almost anything for Young Italy," said Maria."

"Good. We'll leave in five days, but the day before we leave we'll meet with Donatangelo to finalize our plans," said Piero. "He'll give us the money and we'll leave the next morning."

Walking back to the studio after she left, Piero considered how Charles would feel about this. If he discovered Piero was taking Maria on a dangerous operation and worse, if she was hurt or seized by the police, Charles would never forgive him. Piero needed a good explanation for why he was leaving Rome for two or more days.

As soon as Piero walked through the door of the studio an excited Charles said, "You won't believe the size of the marble block I purchased today. I hope I have enough room left in the studio to work."

"It had to be at least a little larger than life-size. Didn't you tell me the couple wanted a life-sized Bacchus?"

"Yes, but the rough block was larger than I imagined. I want to get started on drawings, but need help from my muse. It would help to see other examples of a sculpture of Bacchus, but I know of none in Rome. I've seen engravings of Michelangelo's Bacchus, but unfortunately it's in Florence. Have you seen any?"

"No, but I've seen Bacchus in paintings."

"I could start there. Smyth may be of help. I'll ask him. What have you been up to? I ask only as a formality because I know I'll only get a vague answer from you."

"With friends in Trastevere. When do they plan to deliver the block?"

"In four days. It may cause a major disturbance on Via Sistina. Will you be here?"

"No, but will be back at night. I can't wait to see it."

"Good, I was thinking of having a small celebration in the evening," said Charles. "I thought I'd invite Smyth, Brown, and Winton. Who knows when I'll have a block as large again?"

"That sounds like fun," said Piero. "The next day I leave for a few days."

Charles almost asked where he was going, but knew whatever Piero told him would be suspect.

———

Charles met Maria late in the afternoon and insisted they walk to the Forum. Curious, she asked, "Why there?"

"Because for me it has become the most romantic place in Rome. How can I ever forget watching the sunset together there?"

"I didn't know you had such a romantic side. I'd like to, but it'll be cold."

"Not with you next to me."

"How can I resist."

Charles led her to her special place at the base of the columns of the Temple of Saturn. Resting against a column with Maria in his arms, he said, "I have exciting news. My marble block will be delivered in four days and I can begin carving Bacchus. Only one problem."

"What's that?"

"I have no idea what Bacchus should look like."

"But you did drawings for your clients."

"I did, but they were only a suggestion. I have to make the clay model maquette and need an inspiration. An idea to get me started."

"How about this for inspiration?" said Maria as she kissed him.

"That's a good start," said Charles who returned the kiss. "I was thinking of hosting a small celebration when the block arrives, and I'd like you to come. Who knows when I'll have a block as large again?"

"When?"

"Next week, in four days. Come in the morning. I think you'll enjoy watching them unload this massive block of marble."

About to say yes, she winced. It was the day before she and Piero were leaving for Civitavecchia and they had to meet with Donatangelo. "Oh, I can't come on that day," said Maria.

"Then how about the next day?"

Now, afraid she might say too much, she stammered, "I'm sorry, I can't come then either."

Noticing her uneasiness and the insecure tone of her voice, he said sarcastically, "And the next day?"

Maria now looked like she was about to cry and hesitated before she said, "No."

Puzzled, Charles didn't know what to say next. Was she saying goodbye or leaving him? A sickening feeling overwhelmed him and an uncomfortable silence fell between the two.

Everything, he thought, had been going well. Now this. Where is she going and will I ever see her again? He didn't want to lose her. And then Charles remembered Piero said he would be gone the same days she couldn't come to his studio. Was Maria going away with Piero? Were they lovers in the past and now together once again? No, he never had the feeling they were lovers. Then it occurred to him. Young Italy. They must be doing something for Young Italy. But how could he find out if they were?

Maria put her arms around him and buried her head in his chest. Charles sensed the unspoken message and said gently, "I don't want to lose you. All I can hope for is that you feel the same. I worry about you and your work for Young Italy. Are you going on some sort of secret operation for them?"

She didn't answer but continued to hold him tightly.

He decided to take a chance and said, "Are you going away from the city?"

She sprung from his arms, sat up and looked at him incredulously. "Why do you ask me that?"

"Because Piero has already told me he'll be gone the same days as you. I've told you before I know you two work for Young Italy. I don't want you to continue to put yourself in danger. I worry about you."

"I don't want to lie to you. I love you. Do you understand? Don't ask me anymore questions."

He reached out and pulled her back to him and kissed her warmly. He had his answer and knew it was time to say no more. Pulling her up, he kissed her once more, and they headed back to the studio. He said no more about his invitation to see his new marble block.

Charles couldn't sleep that night. He knew Piero would never tell the truth about what they were doing for Young Italy. He also knew he couldn't stand by and lose Maria because of it. He decided the only solution was to join them. A bold idea, but it might work.

As expected, the arrival of his marble block four days later, created a disturbance on Via Sistina the likes of which had never been seen there before. It took ten oxen to pull the wooden sled up the cobblestone street.

Normal passage on the street was blocked for eight hours. The merchants along the street were furious. There were moments when Charles thought the job would prove impossible, but the ten delivery men never doubted they could unload and move the block into the studio. Standing it upright in the tight studio space was the next perilous adventure, but after a two-hour struggle, they succeeded.

Celebrating this awesome feat of ingenuity and strength was certainly in order. That night, Smyth, Brown, and Winton came to the studio to celebrate. Piero arrived later.

After they drank all the wine his three friends wanted to go to Caffé Greco and continue the celebration, but Piero declined and Charles's had the perfect excuse; it had been a busy day and he could hardly stay awake. He had no intention of letting Piero out of his sight.

As usual, the next morning Charles was up before Piero. There would be time for him to inspect the block for any possible damage during the move from Trastevere. He found no damage. He packed a shoulder bag with what he might need for a short trip and hid it in a corner. When Piero finally came into the studio Charles was working with some clay.

"Has your muse at last come to your rescue?" asked Piero.

"Yes, I think so," said Charles.

"Good, then I expect to see a complete maquette when I return."

"I hope so."

"Remember, I told you I'm leaving for two or three days?"

"I remember. Going anywhere interesting?"

"No, only to Ostia Antica. It'll be nice for a change to breathe fresh sea air."

"*Buon viaggio*," said Charles.

"*Ciao*," replied Piero.

As soon as he was out the door Charles dropped his clay, grabbed his shoulder bag, locked the studio door, and began following Piero, already a safe-enough distance down Via Sistina. Piero headed for Trastevere. After crossing the Tiber River he continued through the Piazza Santa Maria to the cameo workshop, where he and Maria had begun their day delivering the mysterious items in the trunks throughout the city.

Charles stopped about fifty meters from the shop to reconsider what he was about to do. Did he have the nerve to do this and could it put an end to his relationship with Maria? His only concern was her safety.

From where he stood he could see two workers at their benches, but there possibly were one or two more. He remembered she had always gone to the back of the shop behind the stacked amphorae.

Charles approached the shop at a casual pace, took a deep breath, and ran past the astonished workers to the back of the shop. Taken by surprise, they had no time to stop him. Once behind the stacked amphorae he found himself at the top of a stairway leading to what looked like a cellar.

Never hesitating, he ran down the stairs two at a time, followed by two workers who finally caught up with him at the bottom of the stairs and grabbed him. Charles was struggling to free himself when an authoritative voice from the back of the room called out, "Let him go."

After taking a moment to accommodate to the dim light in the cellar, Charles could see Maria and Piero. Both looked dumbfounded. Another man, who had the confident look of someone in charge stood behind a table.

"Charles, what are you doing here, what are you thinking?" exclaimed Maria.

"I can't believe you would do this," said Piero.

"Let's all calm down," said the man behind the table. Pointing to the workers who had chased Charles he said, "You two can go back upstairs. I don't think we'll have any trouble with our uninvited guest. I assume you're Piero's American friend?"

"Yes, I am. How do you know?"

"I know you helped Maria make a delivery and Piero has told me you gave him a place to live after his release from prison. Thank you for both," said Donatangelo. "Now, why are you here?"

"I'm here because I think you are about to send Maria on a dangerous assignment. I can't stand by when I know she may be in danger."

"This none of your business. Please leave Charles. I'll be all right," pleaded Maria.

"I won't go into what you may know about what we do, but she does this of her own free will," said Donatangelo. "We didn't recruit her, she came to us."

"Don't complicate matters. Please leave," said Piero. "Leave now, we'll be all right."

"That's exactly what I suspected. This operation or whatever it is, involves you both. My two closest friends," said Charles angrily. "I refuse to allow Maria to be in danger."

"*Basta, basta*, that's enough," said Donatangelo coming out from behind the table. "Let me handle this. Signor Americano, don't you think it rude to burst into here to tell us what we should or shouldn't do?"

"Not when it puts a defenseless woman in danger. Aren't there any men to do whatever it is you're planning?"

"Donatangelo stared at Charles with a threatening look in his eyes. "Maria makes her own decisions. It's sounding like the only solution to this intrusion is to have my men escort you out. And with force if necessary." As he said this he watched Maria to gauge her reaction. What he detected was these two were in love, and that complicated everything. His planning had become unraveled by an impetuous American. This operation had to proceed as planned. Keeping a large amount of money longer than necessary could only lead to trouble. The longer he had it, the more people found out, and greed often superseded loyalty.

And this American, what to do about him? He didn't impress Donatangelo as a besotted fool. It was likely he had concluded he was dealing with one of the many secret societies of Rome. He knew too much, including where Donatangelo could be found. He had to be controlled.

"Signor Americano, do you mind if Piero and I go upstairs and discuss this problem alone?"

Charles nodded. As soon as Donatangelo and Piero reached the top of the stairs an infuriated Maria approached Charles saying, "How dare you follow me. This is none of your business. Do you have any idea the problems you have caused? I could not believe my eyes…"

"Wait, wait," he said attempting to calm her, but to no avail. His plea only intensified her anger.

"I can take care of myself, thank you," she said waving her arms about in frustration. "This is Rome, not America. Perhaps the women there need coddling, but I don't."

This was a side of Maria he had not seen before. Piero had warned him she could be difficult if challenged. While she paced back and forth in silence radiating fury, Charles loved what he saw, but knew it was no time to argue his case.

Upstairs Donatatangelo said to Piero, "Who would have ever thought we'd be revising a major operation to accommodate an American? But I think it's our only choice."

Puzzled, Piero asked, "You mean the solution is to include him in this trip to Civitavecchia?"

"I think so. It's our only way to keep him under control. If we prevent him from going with you and Maria, he may do something foolish that will harm us even more. He's determined to protect her."

"How do you think she'll feel about that?"

"I watched her as we talked. After the initial shock of seeing the American here, I sensed the fact he came to protect her, touched her deeply. But, of course, she would never give any indication of that to us, and not to him either.

"We have used your friend as a decoy before. At the time I only thought it was a clever idea and never believed it would happen again. But happen it has, and we need this operation to proceed. All the plans with the contact in Civitavecchia have been finalized. No question the American is naïve, but he impresses me as trustworthy and above all willing to do anything for Maria. Do you agree?"

"I agree, but reluctantly. He's a dear friend, but I'd never forgive myself if he gets hurt."

"I'm convinced we have no other choice than to include him. Not only must we complete the operation, we must avoid the risk of him exposing our group. I'm betting on love. They have no intention of losing each another."

"Donatangelo, you surprise me," said Piero. "I've never heard you use the word 'love', and particularly not when it comes to Young Italy."

"Sometimes we must accept a situation for what it is, not for what we would like it to be," said Donatangelo. "Now comes the hard part. Convincing Maria."

They found Maria and Charles sitting in silence about as far apart as possible in the close confines of the cellar.

"I have an idea," said Dnonatangelo. "I have no intention of postponing or cancelling our plans. Your presence Signor Americano, has complicated things. You should know Maria was never in danger. She was asked to accompany Piero because a couple is at less risk of being stopped and searched."

"If you do not want them stopped they must be carrying something illegal," interjected Charles. "That sounds like danger to me."

"Let me finish. Your presence here is dangerous for me," said Donatangelo. "Piero assures me you can be trusted. Because of this, and the fact you're aware he and Maria are already committed to this operation, I think we should allow you to also become part of it."

Maria jumped up and shouted, "I won't allow this to happen. He should not be included."

"If I send him away, I think he'll find a way to follow you, and that puts you, Piero, and our operation in danger," said Donatangelo. "This young man is determined to protect you whether you want him to or not."

Maria did not reply, but Donatangelo and Piero didn't miss the repressed smile as she looked down. Charles said nothing.

"Maria, I think Donatangelo is right. I have no problem with him joining us," said Piero.

The three men waited in silence for Maria to reply. After several minutes she said in a soft, deferential tone "I guess you're right. I agree."

Piero was now responsible for two, instead of one fellow conspirator. A ride in the Campagna with Maria and Charles would under normal circumstances have been a pleasant holiday, but none of the three had any experience in an operation like this.

Emotionally drained by the confrontation in the cellar of the workshop, no one spoke as Piero led them to the carriage barn. There, he encountered his first hurdle. An agreement had been made for two passengers. Three passengers had arrived. As far as the carriage driver was concerned, two meant two, not three. Charles could only smile as he watched Piero and the driver debate the issue from all possible angles. Only in Rome, he thought, could this change in plans result in such a dramatic scene. At last, after Piero had apologized sufficiently for the driver to proclaim a personal victory, and paid the extra fee, the driver agreed to begin their trip.

Maria climbed aboard first, followed by Charles, who hesitated. He looked at her and as she stared out the opposite window. Her message was clear, "Stay away, I'm not ready to talk to you yet." Piero noted this strained unspoken interchange between the two before taking his seat next to Maria, opposite Charles. The driver and his assistant made a final check of the horses and soon they were off.

Maria continued to avoid looking at Charles and no one spoke. His only alternative was to sit back and enjoy the scenery, but after about an hour passed he could no longer contain himself and decided to break the tense silence. "I think it's time for you to tell me what we're about to do."

To his surprise, Piero responded immediately. "First, you should know Maria is carrying ten thousand scudi in her skirt."

"I knew it. This puts her in a most dangerous position."

"You've already made it clear how you feel." said Piero. Maria remained silent as he continued. "This will be our story: Maria and I are accompanying you, our American friend, to Civitavecchia where you will be boarding a ship for Genoa."

"I've always wanted to go to Genoa," said Charles.

"Please, this is serious business."

"But you minimized the danger."

"I thought we were beyond that."

"All right. I understand, and I'll behave."

"Good," interjected Maria. "It's been very difficult for me to accept your presence, no matter how sincere your motives. Now, it's time for us to concentrate on what we're about to do. Piero and I are accustomed to this kind of thing. You must pay attention and follow the plan. That will make us all safer."

Piero added, "It'll be my job to contact a smuggler in Civitavecchia to purchase guns for Young Italy. You and Maria need not accompany me to the meeting with him. Once the purchase is completed and the money transferred, we can leave. I would like to accomplish this as quickly possible."

"How do we find this man?" asked Maria.

"A young boy will contact us at the carriage terminal in Civitavecchia and take me to him. You two can go to a ristorante and wait for me to return. When I return I should have the final instructions for where to deliver the money," said Piero.

"Sounds simple enough, but that makes me nervous," said Charles. "Aren't harbor police always on the lookout for smugglers? This man sounds like a major smuggler. It's hard for me to believe they wouldn't know him."

"Yes, I feel the same way," agreed Piero. "But we must look and act like the others in this city accompanying relatives or friends to board ships. Maria, I feel foolish reminding you, but you must stay as close to Charles as possible. Playing your roll as lovers saying goodbye should help avoid police scrutiny."

The potential for failure sobered Charles. In a short time, he had undergone a metamorphosis from an America sculptor to a Roman conspirator participating in a plot to smuggle guns into the country to overthrow the government. If caught, he could be killed or imprisoned for the rest of his life. The former more likely than the latter.

There was no turning back and too late for doubts or uncertainty. He might be afraid, but he could never bring himself to abandon Maria.

Tired and emotionally spent by the day's unforeseen events, a silence, welcome by all, allowed them the opportunity to doze. Heads bobbed up and down as they slipped into and out of light sleep.

They didn't reach Civitavecchia until after dark. Charles had entered Italy through this port and remembered how excited he was at the time, not knowing what to expect. Entering Civitavecchia once again brought him a feeling of excitement, but this time it came laced with fear. Deep in thought he was startled when Piero announced, "The time has come to begin our adventure. Do either of you have any last-minute questions?" Neither had any questions. Other than the busy carriage terminal, Charles could only remember the harbor and the impressive Forte Michelangelo at the south end of the bay.

Outside, damp sea breeze enhanced the chill from the falling temperature. Charles wished he had brought gloves. Porters were scurrying about loading and unloading luggage from the ships in the harbor. All three looked around for the boy who was to contact Piero, but they had not anticipated the large number of travelers crowding the terminal. How would he find them in this crowd?

After waiting at least twenty minutes it finally occurred to Piero what may have happened. They were now three, not two, as the boy would have been instructed. He asked Maria to walk with him to the edge of the crowd and soon a young boy approached them. They spoke briefly. The boy pointed to a building down the street, and then he and Piero left, heading toward the center of the city, in the opposite direction from which the boy had pointed.

When she returned to Charles, Maria said, "We're to go to the ristorante the boy pointed out and wait there for Piero. I'm hungry, aren't you?"

"Yes, I am," said Charles pleased she was again talking to him. He felt even better when she took his arm as they began to walk to the ristorante. "We still have to find a place to sleep tonight. There should be many hotels catering to the tourists who must spend a day or two waiting for a ship. If we see one should we make a reservation?"

"No, we should wait for Piero. Our plans may change," said Maria. "From here on everything depends on what happens between Piero and the gun dealer."

The young boy took Piero through a mind-boggling maze of streets. The final destination was a three-story stone building wedged between similar stone buildings on a dark narrow street. The boy led him up two flights of stairs to a door, knocked four times, and turned to leave as soon as it opened.

"Wait, wait." said Piero. "I need you to take me back to my friends."

The man who opened the door said, "I'll have someone to take you back. Please come in."

This was not what he expected. The man who opened the door was tall, elegant, and dressed in fine clothes. He assumed it was the dealer who motioned for him to enter. Piero found himself in a spacious room filled with paintings and marble sculptures. He didn't have much time to look around, but his brief scan told him it was a sophisticated art collection.

The man led Piero into another stunning room, a library. Two of the walls were covered from floor to ceiling with books. There must have been at least a thousand. He stepped behind an elaborately carved walnut desk and pointed to a chair saying, "Please sit. You must be tired after your journey." Glad for the opportunity to rest after his long walk from the carriage terminal, Piero sat down in a high-backed chair upholstered in velvet.

"I assume have a letter for me?"

"Yes," said Piero as he fumbled in his shirt to find the envelope Donatangelo had provided him. "Here, it is," he said, as he handed it to the dealer.

The man used a thin knife with a jeweled handle to open the envelope, unfolded the letter slowly, and began reading. He looked up several times as he read and when finished asked, "You're Piero?"

"I am." He doubted the dealer would reveal his own name.

"It says you have ten thousand scudi," said the dealer. "This is a small order."

Ten thousand scudi sounded like a fortune to Piero. "We thought we would begin small and see what it would purchase. If satisfied with the quality, we can begin to buy larger amounts of arms," said Piero, amazed at what he found himself saying. A sudden feeling of self-satisfaction overcame him. Donatangelo had never discussed how to bargain with a dealer, but it seemed to come naturally to him. Perhaps, he thought, it was these rich surroundings that gave him a newfound confidence.

The man held the letter over nearby candle, lit it, and both watched as it burned on a small metal tray on the desk.

"So, we have a deal?"

"Yes," said the man. "My only hesitation is because we have never done business together before. I must be careful. Do you have the money?"

"I understand. But first, I must have a guarantee. A way of proving to our leader how and where the guns will be delivered."

"Your group has been referred to me by the national leader of your organization. I supply guns to his other colleagues in many different cities. You would not ever have found me if he and I didn't have a long relationship.

"As to the delivery, there will be many deliveries made by the farmers who bring the produce to the daily markets in Rome. This has worked in the past. Your leader in Rome knows who to contact for when and where the deliveries will be made."

"I would like to see what we're buying. Can you arrange that?"

"Yes, it's customary for the buyer to see the merchandise," answered the man, "but not before paying me to complete the purchase."

"I don't have the money with me now."

The man looked displeased and paused before saying, "Because this is the first time we've done business, I'll make an exception. You'll pay the man who will let you inspect a sampling of the merchandise. I do not want you to return to this building."

"Where will I find him?"

"A boy will take you to him tomorrow. You'll need a place to sleep tonight," said the dealer.

"Yes. I'll need two rooms."

"I thought you were only two?"

"Originally, yes. Another joined us at the last minute and the third is a woman."

"Stay at the hotel where the boy takes you and in the morning another boy will meet you outside. Only you are to go with him to inspect the merchandise. Remember to bring the money. I think that concludes our business."

He rose and led Piero through the room filled with art, opened the door, and pointed to a young boy sitting on the stairs. "He'll take you back to your friends." Wasting no time, the man quickly closed the door, and left him with the young boy.

On the circuitous walk back to the ristorante Piero was convinced they retraced their steps through the same streets several times. The dealer made certain he covered his tracks. It worked. Piero had no idea where he had been.

The boy took him to a small hotel near the carriage terminal and the ristorante. Before Piero could even say *grazie,* he turned and disappeared into the dark. The entire transaction had all happened so fast he was convinced this was standard procedure for the busy dealer. He had given his customer a brief glance of his lifestyle and riches, assuring him he was indeed an important player in his world. Then he closed the deal, and made certain the customer would never be able to find him again. Piero was impressed.

As soon as Maria and Charles entered the *Ristorante Spiaggia* the aroma coming from the kitchen, told them were in for a treat. Hungry after the long journey from Rome, Maria looked around to see what everyone was eating and pointed to a blackboard that listed the special of the day as *linguini alla scoglio.*

"I don't understand said Charles. "I've never heard of such a pasta."

"It looks good," said Maria. "Look around."

Charles glanced at one of the tables and saw the diners were eating linguini with mussels. He had eaten mussels in Washington and liked them. "It makes sense, we're at the seashore. They should be fresh. Think you'll like it? You were raised on mountain food."

"I've never had mussels but I've heard people talking about how good they are."

"You're about to find out." He asked the waiters opinion, who assured them it was the specialty of the region and the house. *Scoglio,* the waiter said, could mean a reef or a rock. He wasn't sure but, thought it was a southern dialect.

They were not disappointed. The white wine of the region was perfect with the pasta. They ate in silence. Charles thought it best to wait for Maria to initiate any conversation. Her anger in Donatangelo's cellar, and silence during the carriage ride concerned him. Still uncertain if she had forgiven his brash intrusion into her secret world, he didn't wish to reignite her anger.

"Did you enjoy the pasta?" said Maria. "I did. At first the black shells weren't appealing, but after the first mussel went down, I wanted more. The garlic helped," said Maria, breaking the silence with no hint of anger in her voice.

He was ecstatic. The way she looked at him and the pleasant tone of her voice suggested his forgiveness may have begun. "Let's take a walk," suggested Charles. "We can stay near the ristorante so we won't miss Piero?"

Once outside she said, "During that delicious meal I forgot what we were here to do. I won't relax until all this money is out of my skirt and we're in a carriage returning to Rome."

"Let's hope his visit to the gun smuggler was successful."

They walked arm in arm, another indication of his possible return to grace. The dark street was empty and they found a bench in front of a row of high bushes where they could sit and watch for Piero. They were far enough from the ristorante to be out of sight of anyone approaching from the center of the city.

Maria was the first to see him. She recognized Piero's walk. Charles was about to get up and call out to him but she pulled him back down.

"What's wrong?"

"Quiet," she whispered. "Don't move. I think I see somebody following him. Stay still, no one can see us and I want to be certain. Yes, there are two men following him. After he enters the ristorante, we'll wait for a few minutes, then go and meet him inside," whispered Maria. "Let's not move now. I want to see who's following him."

She was right. Two men coming from the direction of the city center emerged from the dark, but stopped when Piero went into the ristorante. They turned and walked back into the darkness.

"I thought so. Let's join Piero."

Maria took his arm and pulled him off the bench and they walked back to the ristorante. Things were happening too fast for Charles to understand or even be afraid. Maria seemed to know what she was doing.

The ristorante was now almost empty. They joined Piero and the waiter who had served them before rushed over, gave them a confused look, and said, "Was the food so good you're already back?"

They laughed and Charles said, "Our friend was delayed. We'll join him for a coffee while he eats."

"We'll be closing in about thirty minutes so please order as soon as possible," said the waiter.

"I'll make it easy for you and order for him," said Maria. "He'll have the *linguini alla scoglio* and we'll have two coffees. Piero, I guarantee you'll like this dish."

"If you say so. I don't have a choice, do I?"

"I was aggressive, probably rude, but Charles will support my choice of pasta. Tell us how your meeting went," she said, looking around to be certain no one was close enough to hear.

"It was nothing like I expected," said Piero in a low voice. "I anticipated meeting a tough looking man in a dark dreary room seated behind a table with a pistol on top. Instead, I found myself with an elegant man in rooms fit for a palace. Our meeting was brief, but successful. Tomorrow, I give the money to one of his assistants after he shows me a sample of his wares."

"Did you know you were followed here?" said Maria.

"No. How do you know?" said Piero, alarmed. "I only walked a short distance from the hotel where I made reservations for the night. Are you sure?"

"Yes. Who took you to the hotel?"

"A boy who worked for the dealer. As soon as we reached the hotel he disappeared."

"We only saw two men walking down the street behind Pierio," said Charles. "Couldn't that be a coincidence?"

"It could, but they turned back after he entered the ristorante. My street instincts tell me something else is going on," said Maria. "I suppose it could be the dealer having you followed to see if you might be working for the police, but I think it's not that complicated.

"Thieves prowl the streets every night in Rome looking for tourists. They wait until an unwary tourist is walking alone in a dark isolated area and rob him, maybe even kill him. Every night there are robberies because the thieves know tourists often carry large amounts of money. With ships coming and going here every day, this is a perfect place to find tourists carrying even larger amounts of money."

"But I don't look like your average tourist," said Piero.

"True," said Maria, "but these thieves may have followed you from the dealer's house. This isn't a large city. The smuggling world is small and thieves have a way of getting such information. To them, if you are here to buy smuggled guns, you must be carrying a large amount of money and an excellent target."

Charles noticed the kitchen door open and nudged her as the waiter approached the table with the pasta and the two cups of coffee. Piero looked down at the pasta, bowed his head toward the plate and inhaled the aroma. He smiled and said, "I think I'm going to enjoy this."

They let him finish his meal, sipping their coffees until he broke the silence. "I don't know what to think. What you say makes sense, but we have no proof. I've made the hotel reservations and we can't sleep here. What do you suggest?"

"We should all walk back to the hotel together, but be prepared for possible trouble. Three walking together may change their plans. I should have a good idea if we are being followed and will let you know as soon as I do. Charles, if there's any trouble let Piero and me lead the defense. You'll be our backup. Wait to see who needs the help and don't panic."

"The pasta was delicious. I'm tired. Let's go," said Piero, standing and walking to the kitchen to find the waiter and pay their bill.

Maria's comment about panicking caused Charles to break into a sweat. He was counting on the possibility their group of three would cancel the plans of the thieves. Untested in any violent situation, he didn't want to disappoint her.

As they left the ristorante, Charles looked around and thought the empty street looked even darker. For him, this all added up to a perfect night for a robbery. Piero led the way toward the hotel and no one spoke as they walked at a normal pace.

The farther they walked from the ristorante, the darker it became. Then, almost on cue, Maria whispered, "We're being followed. Don't walk any faster, but be ready."

Then it began. A man stepped in front of them from a narrow passageway. Charles could see his hand moving into his coat, reaching for a knife or pistol.

Maria didn't hesitate. Before the man could even withdraw his hand from his coat she delivered a vicious kick to his groin. He bent over grabbed his genitals, and falling, wailed in pain. At the same time, she shouted, "Charles jump on him and keep him down! Piero look out behind!"

Piero turned to find a man with a club charging at them. Then all three were stunned when two more men appeared out of the darkness running toward the man about to hit Piero. At first Charles thought they were outmanned, and about to be robbed and worse.

But they watched in amazement as one of the two men who had suddenly appeared, tackled the man about to hit Piero, and in one lightening-like motion slit his throat. The man Maria had kicked was silenced by a blow to the head with a club from the second stranger. Charles would never forget the horror of seeing one man's throat cut and the hideous thud of the club striking the other man's skull, all in a matter of seconds. One of the strangers shouted, "Go on to the hotel. Quick, we'll take care of these two. Move!"

Charles needed no further encouragement. He grabbed Maria's arm and began running. Piero followed and they didn't stop until they reached the hotel. Out of breath they took a few minutes to regain their composure and straighten their clothes before entering the hotel. Inside, Piero calmly asked the man dozing behind the desk for the keys to their rooms and went upstairs.

They all entered the first room. "What was that all about?" said Piero. "Who were those two men or better, who sent them and how did they know what was about to happen?"

"My guess would be your friend the dealer sent them. That was his insurance to protect the money for the purchase of his guns," said Maria.

"Whoever it was, we owe them a debt of thanks," said Charles.

"I think you're right. I told you this dealer was careful. When I told him I didn't have the money with me he looked upset but agreed to the purchase. He must have his men watching whoever visits the house. When the young boy took me back to this hotel they probably followed us and then discovered the thieves following us," said Piero. "I suspect the dealer will have me followed tomorrow when I go to inspect the guns and deliver the money."

"Yes, I think you should feel safe," said Maria "There will also be two fewer thieves on the streets."

"I'll never forget today. Sleep sounds good to me," said Charles, who fell onto the bed as soon as Maria left their room. Piero got in bed and seemed to be asleep as soon as he hit the mattress. But tired as he was, Charles could not sleep. His mind would not let him forget the details of the attempted robbery and murders he had witnessed. The grisly scene replayed in his mind over and over as he tossed and turned.

When he finally drifted off, it seemed only a short time before he awoke, confused and trembling. Had it all happened? Yes, it had. He was about to be killed or at least seriously injured by two thieves. Piero and Maria had taken it in stride or if they were frightened, they didn't show it. Would she be placed in more dangerous situations by Young Italy? Probably. Charles was hopelessly in love with her and wanted to protect her, but knew it would be difficult for her to change her life.

The next morning, they met in Maria's room before going for coffee. "I need the money. Do you have it?" asked Piero.

Maria reached under the mattress and pulled out five wrapped packets the size of paper bank notes. "I slept on them last night."

Handing some money to Charles Piero said, "While I pay for the guns you both should arrange for a carriage to take us back to Rome. We won't have to spend another night here. This should be enough to book a carriage. I'll meet you at the terminal after I finish my business."

"That sounds good to me,' said Charles. "I want to get back to the world I understand as soon as possible."

Frowning, Maria said, "Don't forget, you insisted on joining us."

After they finished their coffee, a young boy approached Piero outside the nearby tratorria and the two headed into the center of the city. Charles and Maria left for the carriage terminal.

The boy led Piero toward the harbor to a typical tourist souvenir shop. The boy told him to go into the shop and examine the seashells on the table in the center of the room.

He did as he was told and began examining shells of all sizes and shapes on the table. As a sculptor, this interested him, and for a moment he forgot why he was in the shop until a man approached and said, "Perhaps I can help you. I have some finer shells in the back."

"I would like to see what you have there," answered Piero.

They walked into a room at the back of the shop and the man said, "The boy identified you as the buyer. The man you met with last night apologizes for the trouble last night. There are always thieves prowling the streets looking for unsuspecting tourists."

"We were most grateful for his help. I was told you had some samples for me to see."

"Yes, let me show you." He moved a few boxes and opened one underneath a pile of others. Inside was an assortment of pistols and muskets. A box next to it contained ammunition.

Piero picked up a pistol and turned it over and over in his hands, then a musket and aimed it at the wall. The truth was he had never fired a pistol, but had fired a musket when he hunted in the mountains and during his Civic Guard training.

"I've been told you purchased ten thousand scudi of muskets, pistols, and ammunition," said the man.

"Yes, that's correct. How soon can we expect the shipment?"

"Your leader will be contacted when the first shipment is about to arrive. As you were told we ship with the farmers who bring their produce to the market. There will be many shipments because of the size of the order, so you should be prepared to visit the market regularly. Sending the entire shipment at one time would too risky."

They shook hands and Piero gave him the money. The man handed him a bag of shells and when he walked out into the street, he looked like the hundreds of tourists who passed through the port each week. In two days, he had never heard anyone's name.

He walked to the carriage terminal and found Maria and Charles. Within an hour they were on their way back to Rome. Now, when Charles stepped into the carriage, Maria made it clear she wanted him beside her.

CHAPTER SIX

Christmas

Returning to his work was the perfect antidote to the fright Charles had experienced during the Civitavecchia escapade. He saw Maria almost daily, and fell deeper in love, but could tell by the sporadic changes in her routine, and thus their plans, that she continued her work for Young Italy. Piero returned to his routine of long days away from the studio and Charles knew it would be useless to try and convince him to once more return to sculpting.

The popularity of Pio Nono continued to increase throughout Rome and the Papal States each day, but had no effect whatsoever on Young Italy's relentless pursuit of revolution. Charles now understood commitment in a new way. He was dedicated to his work as a sculptor and loved what he did. But would he die for his passion, sculpture? That would be ridiculous, but they were prepared to die for Young Italy.

The dreary rainy days of winter encouraged working in the studio. He had found no sculpture in Rome of Bacchus that inspired or motivated him other than the engraving he had of Michelangelo's Bacchus in Florence. Bacchus began to emerge from the marble block. Even Maria sought refuge from the rain and cold in his studio bringing him bread and whatever treat she could find. She would sit for hours watching him work.

One day while in the studio together, Charles stopped working, put his hammer and chisel down, looked up, put his finger over his lips signaling silence, and said, "Did you hear that sound piercing the air? It goes right through me."

After a moment, she said, "That's a *zampognaro*. It's the first I've heard this year. Maybe it means good luck."

"I remember the sound from last year. How can one forget it? Every corner had one. Who are they?"

"The *zampognari* are shepherds from the mountain villages who play bag pipes made from goat bladders."

"Goat bladders. Amazing?"

"Yes, goat bladders. They come to Rome to earn Christmas money, but on their way home pass through the mountain villages serenading the houses. People there may not have money, but give them special foods prepared for Christmas."

He could detect the obvious emotion in her voice as she spoke. He walked to her and thought he could see tears welling up in her eyes.

"You're about to cry, aren't you?"

"I could. Christmas was such a happy time at home. We had little, but my mother did her best to find us candy. Oh, how we looked forward to Christmas."

Taking her into his arms he said, "It hurts me to see you unhappy."

"I'm happy here with you, but I'll never forget my family. The bagpipes resurrected all these emotions. I'll be all right."

Charles continued to hold her and she said no more. He decided this was why he loved her so much. Forged from the necessity to survive without any support when she arrived in Rome, a city notoriously inhospitable to the destitute, Maria had endured. Not only endued but gained the respect of all who knew her.

He began to kiss her, but now with a bold energy rapidly escalating to a level of passion he had not experienced with her before. He knew he couldn't stop and she responded in kind as he had often imagined she might.

As his hands frantically explored the beauty of her body she let out a faint cry of pleasure prompting him to continue his sensuous journey. They began to undress each other as he lifted her and carried her into the back room. They fell onto his bed frantically discarding their clothes.

Now naked before him, he was awed. She was a beauty one could only imagine. His hands ceased to move with frenzied passion and now his fingertips began to lightly caress her soft, warm skin as he gently kissed her breasts, her thighs, her neck, and lips. It was as though they had rehearsed this over and over, each erotic exploration arousing in her a sensuous reply encouraging him to continue. She eased him down and in until they moved as one for a long time transported to the enchanted place inhabited only by lovers, savoring the ecstasy reserved for true lovers.

When spent, they both fell back. He was overwhelmed and temporarily speechless. Maria returned to his arms, kissed him, and pulled a blanket over them.

"I don't think I can express how beautiful you are," said Charles.

"I think you did."

"I've wanted this to happen for so long. Remember when we met in this studio neither of us had the slightest idea we would end up in each other's arms, feeling the way we do. Love and life are unpredictable."

"You didn't, but I did," replied Maria. "I've been alone in the world, discarded by a family because of stupid tradition until I met you. Since leaving my home I've had to live with a deep dark hole in my soul. It's impossible for me to explain how happy you've made me. And now the future. Where will it take us?"

"Then let me bring you back to a life in which you once again become part of a family. Marry me."

She sat up abruptly. Almost jumped up. He couldn't tell if she was about to shout for joy or cry. Struggling to find the right words she finally exclaimed. "You would marry me, the discarded one? Are you certain our beautiful act of love hasn't influenced your thinking?"

"No question it's affected me, but I knew I wanted to marry you before today."

"I know nothing about your family. How do you know if they would accept me, a poor girl from the mountains of a country far away?"

"It'll be a surprise. But I know my mother would be happy if I was happy and pleased to have a new daughter-in-law. My father will be puzzled at first, but he's a quiet wise man who would soon see why I love you and welcome you into the family."

"Do you have any brothers or sisters?"

"Two brothers and two sisters. I'm the youngest and the only one not married. They all live in Washington."

"This is all too much, so unexpected."

"I'm still waiting for an answer."

Now Maria began to cry and between her sobs of joy, said, "Of course I'll marry you."

Piero did not return home that night or if he did he left as soon as he discovered the two lovers asleep in each other's arms. Charles was the first out of bed in the morning and went for two coffees. She was up when he returned and after finishing her cup, she said, "Can we get married now, here in Rome? It would mean so much to me."

"But I'm not a Catholic. I thought that would be against the rules?"

"I've been thinking about that. I was baptized a Catholic. It's hard to explain, but it's still important to me. I know a priest who works with the poor in my neighborhood. He's wonderful, gentle, and kind to everyone and thinks only of others and their needs. When I was desperate and thought I had nowhere to turn for help, he found me work doing laundry. That's how I've survived, making enough to pay for my room and eat. He knows I'm alone and always asks about me. I'm sure he'll marry us."

"What if he asks me if I'm a Catholic?"

"I'll make certain he doesn't."

"This won't get you in any trouble?"

"It shouldn't."

"When were you thinking we should get married?"

"As soon as I can find Father Marco. I hope before Christmas."

"You waste no time."

"Are you changing your mind?"

"No, but it's all coming together fast. I'm used to working slow and deliberately. Each move is carefully considered, so have patience with me. Won't you need a dress?"

"I can't afford a new wedding dress. You'll have to accept me as I am."

"You'll have a new wedding dress," said Charles.

"It's not necessary."

"For me it is," said Charles emphatically. "My bride will have a new dress and we'll take a photograph for my family. I know what a beautiful woman you are and need to show you off to my family and friends in America."

Maria did not know how to respond. A new dress, a photograph. These were things she thought she would never have.

To his surprise, Maria convinced her priest friend to marry them in eight days, exactly one week before Christmas. When he asked her how she convinced him to marry her to a non-Catholic, she told him he never asked. She was almost certain he knew. It would be difficult to keep this a secret in her neighborhood.

Father Marco was a priest who lived and dealt with people who had little or nothing. He understood happiness was a rare gift for them, something to be seized when possible, because it might never surface in their bleak lives again. Maria told Charles he would understand if he lived in her world. To her Father Marco was a great man, a saint.

She found a dressmaker and he made plans for a small celebration after the wedding. Piero agreed to be a witness and a friend of Maria from her building would be the other.

They were married by Father Marco at an eight o'clock Mass the morning of December 18, 1846 on a side alter of Santa Maria della Vittoria at the end of Via Barberini, a Church Charles knew because of its Cornaro Chapel with Bernini's magnificent sculpture, *Ecstasy of St. Teresa*.

He had never attended a Catholic mass and Maria assisted him through the ritual with only one mishap. She forgot about Holy Communion, but when it came time, Father Marco never even looked toward Charles. Oh, how she loved this kind priest.

Charles gave his full attention to Father Marco as he administered the sacred wedding vows. His "I do" came without hesitation as did hers. After the vows she left his side to place a flower at the feet of a statue of the Virgin Mary. She never looked more beautiful to him than she did then, in her new dove-colored wedding dress. He watched his beautiful bride, the committed revolutionary who had faced danger with no fear, gently place the flower and then bow her head in prayer.

He wished he could capture the expression on her face. What, he wondered, do Roman Catholics think when they pray? He had no idea, but he wanted to pray with his wife. He prayed he could love as he knew she would, unconditionally.

Charles hid his misgivings when Maria first mentioned a church wedding. His family were Protestants and suspicious of anything Roman Catholic. He never tried to find a Protestant church in Rome. He assumed there were none. Now that it was over, he was glad she had insisted they marry in church. The civil ceremony following the wedding mass lacked any sense of celebration or permanency.

After the civil ceremony, they went to the photographer. It was a first for Maria, who posed with undisguised pride standing straight, almost rigid next to Charles who was seated with her hand on his left shoulder. The whole process seemed to give her a newfound sense of self-esteem.

When they arrived at the studio Piero and Charles's friends, Smyth, Brown, and Winton had already opened the bottles of wine they had brought to celebrate. They lifted their glasses saluting the newlyweds as they entered. It was a small, but happy party. Later, after the bottles of wine were emptied and the food delivered by the local ristorante consumed, Smyth and Maria's neighborhood friend led all an impromptu dance around the emerging sculpture Bacchus, the perfect guest for such a celebration.

Piero was the last to leave, and as he and Charles embraced, he thanked him for allowing him to stay with him so long. "Remember, I was the one who introduced you to Maria," said Piero.

"I'll always be indebted to you," said Charles. "It's time for you to return to sculpture. Don't let all your talent go to waste. Every time I see you I'll remind you of your gift. Invite us to your new place in Trastevere when you get settled."

"I will," said Piero as he left.

Maria began to collect the glasses and plates, but Charles put his arms around her and walked her to their bed. As the exhausted newlyweds fell to the bed, he said, "That can wait until tomorrow."

So much had changed and so fast. Charles returned to his work and Maria had the first place she could call her home since being ejected by her father. Now that they were married, he thought it would be an appropriate time to discuss her involvement with Young Italy. At dinner one evening he said, "I think we should talk about your work with Young Italy. You've worked hard for Donatangelo, but he uses you as a messenger, not real member of the group. Do they ever listen to what you have to say about the movement?"

She bristled at the comment. "What I do for the movement is important, not necessarily what I say. We have come far and I've had the privilege of being a part of the progress."

"But Donatangelo never hesitates to put you in dangerous situations. As your husband, I think I have to look out for your safety. We're not two individuals going our separate ways any more. I worry about you," said Charles raising his voice.

"I can take care of myself," she said, sharply.

An awkward silence followed as they both looked down at their plates. Clearly affronted by his wife's sharp response, Charles left the table abruptly and went to his studio. He picked up some clay and began to work it, but couldn't concentrate.

Maria cleared the table and began washing the dishes. She had reacted to his questions without thinking and now regretted it. Living on her own for so long had left her unprepared for this new life where decisions sometimes required mutual agreement. She dried her hands, and went to the studio.

When he saw her coming he was surprised and grateful because he knew she was not accustomed to anyone telling her how to live her life. As she had said, she could take care of herself and had for years. He knew it was time for him to back down and before she could say anything, said, "I didn't handle that right. I'm sorry."

"Neither did I," said Maria in a conciliatory tone.

They embraced and kissed. "I have to think about what you said. I never gave a second thought to my participation in Young Italy now that we're married. But I have to agree, it does make a difference. Be patient with me. It has been my life for so long," said Maria.

―――――――――

There was no way one could escape the excitement building throughout Rome for the Feast of Christmas and this would their first together. At least, they both thought so. Then Charles received a message from the headquarters of the Civic Guard, a responsibility he had, in all the joy and happiness, forgotten. He was to report for duty six o'clock Christmas morning.

This would be his first assignment since enlisting and joining him would be Smyth and Brown. They were to report to the gate Porta Pia. Married in a church with one of Bernini's most famous sculptures, Charles was scheduled to spend Christmas guarding a gate designed by Michangelo, the only positive aspect of the surprise order.

After he thought about this, having two Americans and an Englishman on duty Christmas Day, he concluded their commanding officer had found a clever way to avoid assigning three Romans to serve on this major holiday for all families in the city. Assuming the foreign recruits, had no families in Rome, the commanding officer avoided the enmity and probable lengthy vociferous arguments of his native troops pleading, and more likely demanding he change their assignment.

When he showed the order to Maria she said, "Now it's my turn to be concerned for your safety. Why did you join the Civic Guard? It has ruined our Christmas Day and more important, it can be dangerous. You never know when you might be called to back up the Papal troops in a battle, or worse a revolution in Rome. We could be on opposite sides of a fight."

She was right. Instead of impressing her with his enlistment, he had done the reverse, infuriated her. She had made it clear. There was no indication Rome would be attacked, but he could not abandon his two American friends and Piero. He promised he would give this some serious thought, but, for now, their Christmas would have to be celebrated on the 24th.

As was customary in Rome on Christmas Eve, both wore their best clothes. She altered her wedding dress for the feast. They joined the large crowds visiting different churches to view their Christmas decorations, ate roasted chestnuts, and had a glass of warm wine offered by one of the neighbors on Via Sistina.

At nine o'clock they attended the traditional Christmas Eve Mass offered by the pope in the Papal Basilica, Santa Maria Maggiore, filled to capacity with an overflow into the street. The flickering of hundreds of candles produced a show of light and shadow adding to the beauty of the massive marble columns, many sculptures, and paintings adorning the church. Charles's neck began to ache from looking up at all there was to see and admire. At the end of Mass, the *precipio* or crèche on the alter was unveiled for all to worship and admire.

Then back into the streets to see and be seen until midnight when all the church bells in Rome rang, producing an astounding sound, a sound that made one tremble from its sheer power—a stunning bronze concerto. He imagined this would be how the second coming of Christ would be announced. Where else, he thought, but in Rome could one experience such an overpowering performance?

After the delightful late Christmas Eve celebration, reaching Porta Pia the next morning at six o'clock took all the determination Charles could muster. The same could be said for Smyth and Brown who showed the effects of little sleep and too much wine. They were greeted by their superior for the day, an unhappy Roman sergeant who showed little interest in spending his Christmas with these three recruits and let them know it. This would be a long day.

But the spirit of Christmas was on their side. The Romans spent the holiday at home celebrating with their families. Few traveled outside the city, and those coming to Rome for Christmas had already arrived, not wanting to miss the Christmas Eve festivities. And because of the holiday there was no commercial traffic.

After the sergeant spent only ten minutes briefing them on their duties, he retired to the guard quarters to sleep and ordering them to wake him only in an absolute emergency. What constituted an "absolute emergency" had never been made clear, but the three young men in their new uniforms, complemented by the muskets they carried, looked official to anyone approaching the gate. It would have been an ideal day for smugglers and spies, but as far as they could tell, none arrived at Porta Pia.

For the rest of their lives the three would tell the story, embellished of course, of how they alone guarded the city of Rome at the Porta Pia on Christmas Day, 1846.

CHAPTER SEVEN

Margaret Fuller

Donatangelo found a studio for Piero in Trastevere. It served two purposes; first as a reward to Piero for his loyalty and work for Young Italy, and second, as a cover for his participation in the revolutionary activities planned for the new year, 1847. The celebration of Christmas had brought all the group's activity to a halt. Donatangelo asked Piero to join him New Year's Day to discuss his thoughts about the work pf Young Italy for the coming year.

Piero looked forward to the meeting on this cloudy, cold January day. The temperature in Donatangelo's cellar changed little, summer or winter, and would be warmer than his new studio. There was bread, olive oil and of course, wine on his desk and after they raised their glasses Donatangelo said, "To the New Year, *Salute*, and to our cause!"

"Since Pio Nono has lifted many of the restrictions and censorship on their reporting, the newspapers are again interesting," said Piero. "The trouble with the Austrians in the Milan area continues. We should not believe they will be leaving anytime soon, nor should we believe Pio Nono has changed his mind about joining the struggle against them," said Donatangelo.

"What does Mazzini think?"

"He agrees with what I've said. His latest communiqués describe what's happening on the rest of the continent. Running parallel with this outward liberalization in the Papal State is a strong possibility of several revolutions in Europe. The monarchs, particularly in France and Prussia face real threats of revolution. The foreign secretary of England supports this revolutionary activity and has a special dislike of the Austrian empire. His support of Mazzini includes money to bolster our activity."

"Is that where the money for the guns came from?"

"Yes. Even as the other kingdoms north and south of the Papal States continue their attempts to oust the Austrians or their existing corrupt royalty in the hope of unifying Italy, Pio Nono's hands-off policy remains unchanged. For now, he rides a wave of popularity in his kingdom, but if the others in Italy begin to succeed in ridding us of the Austrians, he'll be forced to choose sides."

"And if it happens, what then?" asked Piero.

"Mazzini is counting on Pio Nono to continue to avoid joining the fight against the Austrians. When it becomes clear to everyone he's not on their side, we'll join all the other groups of Young Italy in making the final push for the unification of Italy," said Donatangelo. "For now, we must continue to convince our fellow Romans of the importance of unification. After all, the logical capital of a unified Italy is Rome."

Piero left determined to continue his work for Young Italy, but also to return to his work as a sculptor in his new studio.

Working for two instead of one, and Maria's not so subtle prompting, changed Charles's routine in the studio. He began earlier in the morning and worked until about one in the afternoon, when he stopped for a light lunch with her, followed by a *riposo*. The late afternoons and evenings of winter were too cold to enjoy a *passegiata* allowing him time to work on new clay models. He had never produced as much work in so short a time.

One morning Maria responded to a knock on the door and opening it found a couple she immediately recognized as American by their clothes. The distinguished-looking man appeared to be about fifty, and his wife about the same age.

"What can I do for you?" asked Maria in her best English.

"Is this the studio of Charles Grimes?" inquired the man. "James Winton referred us and we would like to see his work."

"Yes, please come in. He's working, but I'm certain he'd like to meet you," said Maria welcoming them warmly. "Charles, you have some visitors sent by James Winton."

He stopped working, transferred the chisel to his hand with the hammer, brushed the dust off his pants, and came to meet the couple. "Welcome to my studio. I hope you're enjoying Rome?"

"We are, we are," replied the man who introduced himself and his wife.

"Let me take your coats," said Maria. "Can I bring you some wine or tea?"

"Thank you, I'd like some tea," said the wife and the man requested wine.

"Where are you from?" asked Charles.

"Quincy Massachusetts," answered the man. "And you?"

"Washington. But I haven't been home for a long time."

"Washington is growing fast. You may not recognize it if you return. Will you be returning to America?"

"Yes, definitely. I have a large family there. How can I help you?"

"We're interested in purchasing a sculpture and James Winton recommended we visit your studio. He spoke highly of your work," said the man. "What's this you're carving?"

"This is Bacchus who will also be residing in Massachusetts."

"I don't understand how you do this," said the wife. "How do you know where to begin?"

This was Charles's cue to promote his work. He always began by showing the clay model he had made first, and all the other models he had made, pointing out the major features that emphasized the theme of each work. Today, he was working, a good way to impress a possible client.

He walked back to the marble block and continued carving where he had left off, the right arm of Bacchus. He worked for a good ten minutes defining the biceps area. The couple watched intently, fascinated by the emergence of an upper arm from a nondescript block of white marble. Charles put his chisel and hammer down when he saw Maria bringing chairs for the visitors and the tea and wine with *biscotti*.

"Do you have something in mind?" he asked the couple as they sat down to enjoy the refreshments.

"We both love music," said the wife. "We have nothing specific in mind. Could you suggest something, not as large as your Bacchus, but about half-life size?"

"I can. How long do you plan to be in Rome?"

"Another ten days," answered the husband."

"Fine, I'll make some drawings, and from them, make a clay maquette, a clay sketch. If you come back in a week, it should be ready and if you're interested, I'll send a photograph of the final model when it's completed. My terms are typical of the other sculptors in Rome. Half the price up front and the remainder on delivery. I pay for the shipping."

The gentleman asked the price and Charles gave him an estimate, saying he would be able to give him a firm price after he completed the clay sketch. The couple looked satisfied.

Charles and Maria spent the next hour chatting with their guests about Rome, their travel experiences, and their interests in music. After they left he told Maria, "You did a good job. A definite improvement over my handling of previous referrals from Winton. Alone, I was clumsy and didn't know how to speak to possible clients. Adding the refreshments was a great idea."

"I enjoyed meeting the American couple. You'll never visit an Italian home without tasting food and wine," she said. "It comes natural. Are there many American sculptors in Rome? Brown is the only other one I've met."

"There are and I know Winton also refers American tourists to their studios. He's been good to all of us. I need the referrals more than some of the others who have good connections in America. William Storey is, like Brown, from Boston, and the son of a United States Supreme Court justice. Brown told me he frequently entertains American visitors.

"Another is Thomas Crawford who came to Rome, as I did, with no money. Then he met and married an heiress from New York. He has a busy studio and lives in a palazzo. A success story in more ways than one, but he's a good sculptor."

"I'm confident you can compete with any sculptor In Rome or anywhere else," said Maria. "Now I know what to have on hand before the next possible client's visit."

The couple from Quincy did return and approved Charles's clay sketch of a young boy playing a recorder. He also gave them the preliminary drawings he had made for the clay maquette.

Maria became an important partner in Charles's sculpture business and Winton's referrals of American tourists to the studio resulted in two more commissions. With the upfront money of these three and the final payment having arrived for his first commission he could afford a larger studio.

Convinced that his wife had a special talent and charm for dealing with people, he asked Maria to search for a new studio. Within two weeks she found one about fifteen minutes away from his current studio and close to the Piazza Del Popolo.

Recently vacated by a French sculptor the studio space was the size Charles needed. It had good lighting and one wall had double doors that opened to the central courtyard of the building. The best part for Maria was the bonus of a four-room apartment above the studio. Two weeks later they began moving into their new home. By then it was mid-February and the first buds were appearing on the sycamore trees lining the nearby Via Del Corso.

In early March, Donatangelo received word from Mazzini that his friend, journalist Margaret Fuller, was touring the Naples area and planned to be in Rome by the end of the month. He asked Piero to visit Maria to see if he could convince her to assist Fuller.

Piero had no trouble finding the studio. When he first knocked no one answered but he was not about to walk away after his long walk. He continued to knock until he heard a familiar voice from above shout, "Piero, I'll be right down." When the door opened Maria hugged him, and said, "I'm so glad to see you. He's working and didn't hear you knocking."

She led him into the studio where Charles, absorbed with his carving, didn't hear them approaching. Piero tapped him on the shoulder, he jumped, and turning around was surprised to see his old friend. The two embraced and Charles put down his tools and said, "Welcome to our new home."

Looking around Piero said, "I'm impressed. What a fine studio space. And all these marble blocks. It seems you have more commissions."

"I do. The move was hectic, but we have things under control and can now return to seeing our friends. It has taken a month to get settled."

"I saw Winton at the Caffé Greco and he told me about your new commissions."

"He's the one who refers the tourists to me. I don't know how to thank him.".

"Make him a portrait bust in marble. I'm certain he'd be flattered."

"What a good idea," said Maria and Charles nodded in agreement. "Let me show you our apartment."

Maria's pride was obvious. Walking through the rooms, she told him where she had purchased each piece of furniture and what bargain prices she had paid for them. She then insisted they sit at their new table while she opened a bottle of wine and cut some bread and cheese.

"*Buona fortuna!*" said Piero as they raised their glasses.

"Thank you," said Charles. "Tell us what you've been doing."

"I now have a small studio and am working in clay. When I finish a piece I like, I'll put it in marble."

"About time. I know you never tell me much, but I assume you're still working with Donatangelo."

"No, I won't tell you much, but that's why I'm here. Maria, Donatangelo asked me to enlist your help with a special visitor coming to Rome at the end of the month."

"You want us to have him stay here?" asked Maria.

"No, no. It's a woman and this is a special request from Mazzini," said Piero.

"Who is this woman and why is Mazzini so interested in her?" asked Charles.

"Her name is Margaret Fuller. She's a journalist who writes for an important newspaper in New York City. Mazzini thinks her articles will help influence the Americans to support our case for unification. He has already convinced many in England to support his work. They not only support the unification, they give him money."

"What do they want me to do with this woman? Is she married?"

"She's not married and we don't know the exact date she's arriving, but it will be at the end of the month, around Easter. At the moment she's touring the Naples area. Apparently, she's traveling with American friends and will be staying with them until she finds an apartment in Rome. Donatangelo would like you to be available to help after Easter. Are you willing to do this?"

"Yes," said Maria without hesitation. "This will be different. It sounds interesting."

"And safe," said Charles enthusiastically.

"You mentioned Easter. We would like to invite you to join us for Easter Sunday dinner. We'll also be inviting Smyth, Brown, and Winton. Can you come?" asked Maria.

"Thank you, I'd love to," said Piero. "I miss my family on the holidays, but now you're my family in Rome."

Piero returned two days later to let Maria know they had heard from Mazzini. Margaret Fuller would be arriving in Rome on Palm Sunday. She was to find a small apartment that could be available the Monday after Easter. Fuller would be living alone.

Italy was to be the last stop on Margaret Fuller's European journey, and Rome, a city she was eager to see. Her carriage was delayed at the Porta San Sebastiano gate due to a combination of pilgrims walking to Rome for Easter, and a long line of carriages. Her traveling companions in Italy, the Springs from Boston, were as irritated as the carriage driver. Tired from a long day of travel, this delay added to their weariness.

The cheerful spirit of the pilgrims was, for Margaret, contagious. Some were singing psalms as they waited. She would have preferred to walk alongside the carriage and join the animated crowd as it made its slow passage toward the gate, but that could embarrass the carriage driver and the Springs.

The Springs had leased an apartment near the Spanish Steps, an area favored by English and American tourists. By the time they reached the apartment and unloaded the luggage, it was late and they were ready for bed, but Margaret had one last thing to do before retiring. She needed to find a note in her most important piece of luggage, her portable writing desk.

She opened it, pulled up a chair, and began searching the small drawers looking for the note Mazzini had given her in England. That was a long time ago—exactly how long, she couldn't remember. She had been traveling for over three years. Time had become blurred by the constant moving, sight-seeing, and dinners leaving her exhausted.

The note had instructions on how to contact the person who would provide her with assistance in finding an apartment. It took a while, but she found it, relieved she had not misplaced it. The next morning, as the note instructed, Margaret had the building concierge deliver an envelope to the Trastevere address specified by Mazzini. Later that day she received an unsigned note saying a woman named Maria Grimes would come to see her the Monday morning after Easter. 'Grimes', thought Margaret. Not exactly an Italian name.

The next day the three began their exploration of the city and their spirits improved. As they walked, they could hear people speaking French, Spanish, German, and other languages of the continent. All had gathered in Rome to take part in the Holy Week ceremonies culminating in the Papal Mass at St. Peter's Basilica on Easter morning, followed by the annual Papal Blessing.

Vendors sold colored Easter eggs throughout the city. She marveled at the amount of energy created by all the pilgrims crowding the streets in anticipation of the feast of Easter. At home, in America, Easter was an important holiday, but Christmas was a bigger celebration.

There was a service held in the Sistine Chapel called Maundy Thursday that sounded interesting to Margaret and the Springs. It would give them an opportunity to view Michelangelo's magnificent fresco and attend a Roman Catholic Mass, something Margaret had never done.

On Thursday they set out for the Sistine Chapel but as soon as they reached the street outside their apartment faced their first obstacle.

The passing carriages were filled with others headed in the same direction. It took at least twenty minutes to find an empty carriage and before the driver would proceed they had to agree to an inflated price that he attributed to the 'holiday rush'.

Their original plan was to leave early and enjoy a stroll in St. Peter's square, but they were already behind schedule. The line of carriages and walkers attempting to enter the square caused further delay. Carriages jammed the square. Not wanting to miss the opening procession of the Pope and the accompanying clerics, they decided to abandon the carriage and walk the remaining distance.

Everyone else had the same idea, and the closer they came to the Sistine Chapel the more crowded it became. People began to rush. Soon they were trapped in the throng intent on entering the chapel. Margaret lost sight of the Springs as she was engulfed by the surging crowd and pushed forward toward the only door to the chapel. Unable to free herself, she became frightened.

The final push of the crowd as they squeezed their way through the door of the chapel was terrifying. Margaret could barely breathe and had no control over her movements as she was propelled through the door by the frantic hoard of zealots. Once inside and able to walk on her own, she stopped to see if she still had her purse and if her dress was torn. Finding everything in order she worked her way as close to the altar as possible, but still did not see the Springs.

The magnificent surroundings calmed her. Lit by a multitude of candles surrounding, and on the altar, Michelangelo's fresco was stunning, a suitable reward for her frightening entrance to the chapel. But her opportunity to view the ceiling was soon interrupted by the entrance of the papal procession from a door behind the altar.

First came the cardinals, with their red caps and slippers followed by the Mass celebrants in elegantly embroidered purple vestments. Pio Nono entered last. Margaret followed him as he moved about the alter. He impressed her as a good choice for the role he had to play. Confident, yet gentle in manner, and comfortable in his part of the

112

ritual. Her first impression of the man, admittedly superficial, was favorable.

The celebration of the mass confirmed what she had heard. No other religious group could equal or exceed the rituals of the Roman church. An unexpected surprise was the ceremonial washing of the feet of twelve peasant men, an obvious homage to the twelve apostles. At the end of the service Margaret made no attempt to leave. She wanted to spend additional time studying Michelangelo's fresco and, more important, avoid the chaos of the exiting crowd.

Only a few remained in the chapel when she had decided to leave. Outside, the Springs were nowhere in sight. She paced back and forth in front of the basilica and then walked up to the top of the steps where she could see across the entire square. It didn't help. Soon the carriages were gone, leaving her wondering how she would get home. She remembered the name of the street, but had no idea in which direction to begin walking to the apartment.

Coming down the stairs she noticed a young man watching her, and when she reached the square he walked up to her and said in broken English, "I've been watching you. You look lost. Perhaps I can help you?"

She was taken by surprise by this tall, thin, young man with a sharp Roman nose, who appeared to be in his twenties. It was the middle of the afternoon and there were many people still entering and leaving the basilica, so she felt safe. Before she could reply, he added, bowing slightly, "Let me introduce myself. I am Marchese Giovanni Angelo Ossoli."

No question she was flattered by this offer and introduction from the handsome Roman aristocrat. Almost certain she would get lost attempting to find her way home by herself, she conceded, "I am lost. I've only been in Rome for a few days and have become separated from my friends. I know the name of my street, but the carriages are gone. Perhaps you can tell me how to find my way?"

"What is the name of your street?" asked Ossoli.

"It's near the Spanish Steps. If I get there, I think I can find my way to the apartment," said Margaret.

"I can help you," said Ossoli. "Come, I'll show you the way."

"Please, Marchese, I don't want to interfere with the rest of your afternoon. Point me in the right direction and tell me the name of the major street I should follow after I cross the Tiber River," she said half-heartedly. There was something about him that intrigued her.

"You do not have to call me Marchese. Giovanni or Ossoli would be fine. "I cannot allow you to walk alone. It would be improper and could be dangerous for a you walking unescorted on the streets of Rome. And it would be my pleasure to introduce you to the sights of Rome along the way. Please, allow me, though it will be a long walk."

Margaret had forgotten about that ridiculous custom in Rome—the necessity for proper unmarried women to be escorted while out on the street—but he was right and pleased she now had an appropriate excuse to accept his offer. She replied, "*Grazie*, Giovanni. I would be grateful if you escorted me home."

The combination of the pleasant spring afternoon and Giovanni's charm and running commentary on the historical background of the sights of Rome captivated her. Once they were across the Tiber she noticed empty passing carriages, and he must have also, but neither suggested they hire one for the remainder of the journey.

When he led her into the Piazza Navona, she stopped, looked up and down the length of the long narrow piazza and smiled. He noticed her reaction and suggested they sit at one of the outdoor trattorias and have coffee.

"I would love to," said Margaret, who had not eaten since breakfast.

He chose the tratorria across from Bernini's *Fountain of the Four Rivers*.

She had not sat down since before leaving for the Sistine Chapel and when Giovanni ordered, she asked if he could also order her a small sandwich. Resting in the afternoon shade and looking at the magnificent Bernini fountain with the church behind, the obelisk in the center, and the other fountain at the opposite end of the piazza, awed Margaret. Giovanni said nothing.

When the waiter arrived with the coffees and sandwich, Giovanni said, "This is my favorite piazza. I could see you were enjoying the setting. Rome has many other beautiful piazzas and I would be pleased to show them to you."

Margaret did not reply immediately. She felt relaxed with this man, free to be herself and not the center of attention, always on stage, as she often was at her lunches and dinners, while she traveled. No clever talk, no great ideas or problems to debate. She needed time alone, time to write uninterrupted by an often-boring social life. From what she had seen so far, Rome would be the perfect place to fulfill this need.

"I'm sorry, Giovanni, don't misinterpret my silence. It has been an astounding day and this is a delightful introduction to this city," said Margaret gesturing with her hand around the piazza.

"Then allow me to show you more of my city," said Giovanni looking intently into her eyes. "There is much to see and enjoy."

"I think I would like that," she replied softly, then more quickly and firmly, "I know I would."

When they reached the apartment, both found it difficult to part. After an awkward silence, Giovanni said, "When can I see you again?"

Without hesitating, Margaret replied, "How about Easter Sunday morning."

"What time?"

"The Papal Mass is at ten. Why don't you come by at ten?"

"We would be late for the service."

"I don't wish to go to the service, but my friends are planning to go. I would prefer to take a walk and see more of Rome."

"I'll be here at ten," said Giovanni with a bow as he kissed her outstretched hand.

Once inside, she stopped, leaned back against the wall of the entryway, and assessed the events of the afternoon. She was thirty-seven and Giovanni looked ten years younger. Was she blinded by his charm?

She had encouraged his attention, but her American friends would see this as a foolish flirtation with a young Roman aristocrat no match for her brilliance and international reputation.

She prepared answers to the questions the Springs would probably ask. She was not going to change her mind about seeing Giovanni on Easter Sunday morning and the day after Easter she would be moving to her own apartment. Any future liaisons would be out of their sight.

When she entered the apartment, the Springs rushed to the door wanting to know what had happened and where she had been all this time? Margaret told them she had remained in the Sistine Chapel after the service admiring Michelangelo's fresco, and when she could not find them, decided to tour the Basilica of St. Peter. Fascinated by what she saw, she had lost all sense of time. Then she hired a carriage and returned home.

———————

Easter Sunday fell on the first Sunday in April, early spring and perhaps the loveliest season in Rome. Maria had two objectives for the week before Easter. First, she found a possible apartment for Mazzini's friend, Margaret Fuller, five minutes from theirs.

She spent the rest of the week preparing for Easter dinner, her first, and the first in their new apartment. She planned a traditional Easter meal beginning with pasta in a tomato sauce typical of her region, then lamb served with artichokes, and for desert, *Colomba di Pasqua*, a traditional cake in the shape of a dove.

Charles had watched with interest as Maria transformed their apartment into a home. He had come to Rome to study sculpture and never considered what life might be like after his apprenticeship. Art had a way of seducing its impassioned believers and blinding them to the notion there could be any happiness beyond its substitute for living, its studios and galleries. He had no desire to abandon sculpture, but married life had changed him.

William Smyth, was the first guest to arrive on Easter with a large bouquet of flowers in hand. Piero brought twelve *maritozze*, buns filled with sugarcoated pignoli or pine nuts, a Lent specialty. Everett Brown and James Winton came with bottles of wine. The party was off to a good start and after they had all finished complimenting Maria for her excellent taste in furnishing her new home they sat down for dinner at the table decorated with a centerpiece of colored Easter eggs.

With a broad smile, a proud Charles rose, raised his glass and said, "*Salute! Buona Pasqua*," and so began the first dinner with friends at their apartment.

There was little talk during the first course, which the bachelor guests ate with obvious delight. In the pause before *piatti secondo,* or second plate, Smyth pointed to the colored Easter eggs and said, "The past two weeks every corner in Rome had someone selling colored eggs. The tradition puzzled me so I did some research and found several different reasons. They all, in one way or another, had the egg representing a beginning. In the Middle East eggs represented the beginning of their new year, which coincided with the spring equinox. For the Catholics, it's a beginning of a new church year."

"No more wine for Smyth," interrupted Brown. "He's probably the only person in Rome who needed an explanation for why we have colored Easter eggs. Everyone else is content with the idea they are decorative and more inviting to eat than the plain hard-boiled egg." They all had a good laugh as Brown took one of the eggs, cracked and peeled the shell, and downed it in two bites.

As Maria entered the room with the lamb and artichokes, they all clapped. "Charles you are a lucky man to have so fine a cook. If I knew her cooking was that good, I would never have introduced her to you," said Piero.

"Too late Piero," said Charles.

"Everett, I forgot to tell you. Margaret Fuller is in Rome," said Winton. "She stopped at my office yesterday."

"Where's she staying?" asked Brown.

"With her Boston friends, the Springs, until she finds a place of her own," answered Winton.

Piero, Maria, and Charles exchanged brief furtive glances, but gave no indication they recognized Fuller's name.

"My family wrote me she would be stopping in Rome. When I met her in Boston she was with Ralph Waldo Emerson," said Brown. "She spent a great deal of time with him. Sort of a protégé and a major disciple of his Transcendentalist circle. She's probably the most important woman writer in America and, to the dismay of most men, a major advocate for women's rights."

"What does Transcendentalist mean?" asked Piero.

"Let me try to explain. If anyone has a better explanation, please interrupt me. My understanding is they feel people are inherently good and best left alone. They become corrupted by any attempt to organize them or guide them," said Brown. "Anyone have a better description? I'm certain it's much more complicated, but that should give you an idea of the basis for their beliefs. Emerson has a big following in the New England area of America."

"That's in direct contrast to the Papal States where everything people do is guided by the pope. If this journalist attempts to convert Romans I doubt she'll be welcome here for any length of time, both by the pope and Italian men," said Piero.

"You're right, but she told me she was touring England and the continent on assignment for Horace Greeley's *New York Tribune* to report on the dramatic political changes occurring on the European Continent and Italy. Emerson is not with her," said Winton.

"It'll be interesting to see what she writes," said Brown. "Margaret Fuller is a brilliant woman and, will no doubt find fascinating stories to send back to the *New York Tribune*. I know the Springs and will stop to see her."

The wine disappeared almost as fast as the lamb and artichokes. Maria gave her guests a long respite and Charles opened all the shutters before she served the traditional Easter *Colomba di Pasqua* cake. Cups of coffee and the fresh spring air helped revive the satiated guests.

"James, you receive newspapers from home and talk to American tourists. What's happening at home?" asked Brown.

"We're at war with Mexico. The Mexican soldiers have been driven from the territory of California and we've now invaded Mexico," said Winton.

"War in America, fighting the Austrians in Italy, a possible revolution in France. Is there peace anywhere?" asked Charles.

"At the moment peace is difficult to find," said Winton. "Pio Nono has calmed the Papal States with his liberal reforms. His people are as happy as I've ever seen them."

"But we're still a fractured peninsula. Pio Nono has done nothing to mend the divisions between the kingdoms or support the efforts for the unification of Italy," interrupted Piero.

"Mazzini never ceases to remind us all of that," said Winton. "Without the help of the Papal States unification appears impossible. Do you think Pio Nono will ever change his mind about fighting the Austrians?"

"We'll never give up on the idea," reiterated Piero. As he said this he noticed Maria's disapproving frown and interpreted this as a signal for him to say no more.

"Unification of multiple kingdoms or colonies, as happened in our revolution in America, is possible. You have the necessary intellectual leadership, but no strong military leader has emerged," said Brown.

"I assume you're speaking of Mazzini as the intellectual force of this movement," said Winton. "Years ago, Mazzini was banned from Italy when he and a man named Garibaldi led an uprising in the Piedmont region. When it failed, Garibaldi fled and was sentenced to death in absentia."

"Where is he now?" asked Smyth.

"He fled to Brazil and has been active as a mercenary in Uruguay," said Winton.

"Does that mean he'll never return to Italy?" asked Smyth.

"From what I've heard he wants to," said Winton.

"Enough about revolution and fighting, we have this wonderful cake to taste," said Charles who raised his glass and said, "*Salute!*"

At the end of the afternoon, when the others had left, Piero handed Maria a piece of paper and said, "Here's where you can find Margaret Fuller. Have you found an apartment for her?"

"Yes, and it's close to ours," said Maria.

"Good. It should be interesting for both of you."

"I'm nervous. I've never done anything like this."

"I have complete faith in your ability to handle anyone," Piero assured her. "Let me know if you need any help."

On Easter morning, Margaret told the Springs she had an upset stomach and would not join them for their visit to St. Peter's Square and the Papal Mass. They were disappointed, but understood, and left about 9:30. Knowing they would be gone at least three hours she prepared for her visit with Giovanni.

He was on time and she did not keep him waiting. The spring morning couldn't have been more beautiful as he walked with her to the Pincio gardens. At ten in the morning on Easter Sunday, most Romans were in Church and the two were almost alone as they strolled on the deserted streets.

He explained the history of the area, but what touched her most was the ambience of the morning—the fresh spring air and gardens, all accentuated by the presence of this indulgent young man.

When they stopped for coffee she said, "You have a title. Tell me about your family."

"The Ossoli family have always supported the papacy and still do. My father and my two brothers have positions in the government of the Papal States. The family association with the papacy has existed for generations."

"And you also work with them?"

"No, and I hope I can trust you when I say I'm not a supporter of the pope. I recognize him as our spiritual leader but not as our temporal leader. This makes me the black sheep of the family and as the youngest son, am treated as such."

"You can trust me."

"The aristocracy in our family have clear rules of succession and because I'm the youngest of three sons, about all I'll inherit is my title."

"I hope you didn't interpret my curiosity as impolite or prying into your personal life."

"Since you are not a Roman, I did not want you to have any false impressions about my title."

Margaret was touched by his humility and honesty, rare qualities in most of the upper-class people she had met in her travels. When they ended their walk, he asked, "May I see you again soon? You have made this an Easter I'll not forget."

Blushing she said, "And you have made mine special also. Yes, Giovanni, I would like to see you again. Tomorrow I'm supposed to be shown an apartment. I'll be living alone and will leave my new address with the building concierge where I am now. Check with him Wednesday."

On Monday morning Maria had no idea what to expect as she climbed the stairs and knocked on the door of the address Piero had given her. It was opened by a woman who looked to be about forty, with auburn-colored hair pulled back into a tight bun. Taller than the typical Roman woman, she said, "You must be Maria Grimes?" Please come in."

"Yes, I am, and you're Margaret Fuller?"

"I am. *Con piacere*," said Margaret. "I understand you came to help me find an apartment?"

121

"I've already found one you may like. It's close and we can walk there."

"Perfect," said Margaret, anxious to be on her own. "Let me get my wrap and we can leave right away."

While they walked Margaret said, "Your name is Grimes, but you speak English with an Italian accent."

"My husband is American, but I could not be more Italian. He came here to study sculpture and found an Italian wife."

"How interesting. I know there are other American sculptors in Rome. Does he have a studio?"

"Yes, and it's five minutes from this apartment I'm going to show you."

"How convenient. I must stop to see his work."

"Please do. It will also make it convenient for me to go back and forth to your apartment," said Maria.

They spent the next half hour inspecting the apartment north of the Piazza del Popolo. Margaret liked the location, the furnishings, and most of all, the low price. It would be the perfect place to begin her stay in Rome and to write.

"How often will you be available to accompany me around Rome?" asked Margaret.

"Most days. Because I'm only ten minutes away I can also be available on short notice."

"I'm anxious to get settled. I can have my things brought here this afternoon. Let's go back to my friends' apartment and get started. Will you be able to help me get organized today?"

"Yes, of course," answered Maria.

At the end of the day when Maria returned to the studio, Charles stopped working and said, "Tell me about this mysterious journalist. What's she like?"

"I like her. All business, knows what she wants, and impresses me as highly intelligent. She would never be mistaken for a Roman woman of her class. She dresses fashionably, but not to stand out, and has a strong personality. Perhaps too strong for most Roman men. I think I'll learn a great deal from her."

"Your personality needs no strengthening," laughed Charles who returned to his work.

Free to help him and his sculpture business the two became a team. Maria received potential buyers referred by James Winton allowing Charles to devote more time to his work. The result was more commissions and the necessity to rent even additional studio space in the neighborhood. He hired two Italian carvers to do the roughing out or outlining of his new commissions, saving him a great deal of time and effort. The American dollar was strong in Rome and he and Maria could afford a lifestyle neither had ever imagined before, but they continued to live modestly.

With all this new work, fulfilling his duties with the Civic Guard became difficult. Fortunately, they were considerate of their expatriate troops using them almost exclusively for duty at the gates of Rome. However, the thought he could be activated for an emergency or to leave Rome, to fight elsewhere, never left Charles's mind.

It became particularly upsetting whenever Maria returned from meetings of Young Italy and told him about the perpetual discussions of their cause. He hoped he hid is anxiety, because, Charles knew that unification of Italy was unlikely to happen without bloodshed.

Working with Margaret was different from anything Maria had ever done. In the evening she would tell Charles where they had been each day, who they met, and what they talked about. She needed his help to make sense of the complicated ideas being discussed.

Something she did not discuss with him was the presence of a man who introduced himself to her as Marchese Giovanni Angelo

Ossoli. Perhaps ten years younger than Margaret he visited her every day. The two were inseparable.

One morning when she arrived as Ossoli was leaving the apartment. Margaret waited until he was gone and said to the embarrassed Maria, "It's obvious isn't it? I'm in love."

"I'm happy for you both," said a relieved Maria.

Margaret explained how they met and how happy she had been with him. Then she said, "I'm not trying to impress you, but I'm somewhat of an important literary personality in America and an advocate for women's rights. That's a cause important to me."

"And to me," interrupted Maria.

"I detest gossip. My American friends here in Rome would have a difficult time understanding my relationship with Giovanni. I love him because he's Giovanni, only interested in my happiness, and not someone important to my career. It would perplex my friends. That's how they think."

"It makes sense to me. If you believe in women's rights, your relationship with Giovanni is for you to decide, not your family or friends." said Maria. "I never had that right. Few women in Italy do. Not having any rights as a young woman disrupted my life. For a time, I was forced to fend for myself on the streets of Rome. Nothing can be more demeaning."

"I'm sorry, I didn't know."

Maria then told Margaret about the unjust ejection from her family. Shocked by the autocratic power of her father, Margaret said, "That's what the women's movement is all about in America. I wish I could say we are close to equality with men, but the truth is, we're struggling and have made little progress. Now I know you understand my predicament and know I can trust you not to tell anyone. I'll reveal my relationship with Giovanni when I think the time is appropriate."

Avoiding the active social scene of the American tourists and expatriates gave Margaret a chance to write every day. At the end of each day she would read what she had written to Maria who marveled at her talent and considered it her lesson for the day. She had only spent three years at a church school taught by the nuns. In that short time, she only learned to read and write.

At the end of one of these sessions Margaret said, "I'd like to meet your husband and see his studio."

"He'd like that. Why don't you come for dinner? I love to cook. Bring Ossoli. I have not told Charles about him. I know if I explain the difficulty of your situation he'll understand."

She did not reply immediately, taking her time before answering, "I think Giovanni and I would like that."

The next night, when Charles opened the door, he smiled and said, "Lieutenant Ossoli, I'm surprised and pleased to welcome you to my home."

"Thank you, and may I introduce Margaret Fuller," replied Ossoli.

Looking puzzled Margaret said, "Obviously you two know each other. Why?"

"We're both in the same company in the Civic Guard," said Ossoli. "We see each other regularly at the training exercises."

"Yes," said Charles, "and congratulations on your recent promotion to Lieutenant."

Margaret and Maria looked at each other in astonishment and then burst into laughter. "What a pleasant surprise," said Margaret. "I've heard so much about you Charles, and your work."

"I'm sure Maria has exaggerated my ability as a sculptor, but I wouldn't have it any other way," he said laughing and putting his arm around her. She looked relieved.

While Maria finished preparing their meal, Charles took Margaret and Ossoli downstairs to his studio. Margaret was fascinated by his explanation of the process of creating a marble sculpture and thought it might make an interesting story for one of her dispatches to the

New York Tribune. When he finished, Margaret said, "Your work is impressive. Would you mind if I feature you in an article for the newspaper about the life of an American Sculptor in Rome?"

It didn't take long for him to reply "Not at all. I'd be flattered."

They had a pleasant dinner and evening together. Charles and Ossoli spent the night discussing Civic Guard training and duty. Before they left Margaret said, "This has been a delightful evening. I wish we had done this earlier. Maria, I promised the Springs I would accompany them to Milan and Venice. They want to leave next week. It's earlier than I expected and we'll be gone for two months."

Maria glanced at Ossoli to see his reaction to what Margaret had said. It was plain to see he was unhappy, but said nothing. "What about the apartment?"

"I've been renting it by the month. I think I'll let it go and store my things at the Springs. Giovanni and I were trying to find a way for him to receive my letters. Would you mind if I addressed them here?"

"That would be no problem."

After they left, Maria said, "What a surprise for Margaret and me. You should have seen her expression when you greeted Ossoli by name."

"At Easter, Brown said she was an important literary personality in America. As you said, she's both intelligent and confident. Don't worry, I won't say anything about our dinner, but Smyth and Brown know Ossoli is a member of the Civic Guard. They wouldn't be surprised if I knew him."

At the next training session, Piero saw Charles talking to Ossoli and joined them. Saluting he said. "Lieutenant, allow me to introduce myself, I'm Private Piero Cifaldi, a friend of Private Grimes. Congratulations on your promotion."

"Thank you. I'm trying to meet as many of the company as I can, but it will take time," said Ossoli. "It's about time for formation. Please excuse me."

As Charles and Piero walked toward the rest of their platoon Piero said, "How did you two meet?"

"We met here" said Charles, remembering his promise to keep Margaret's secret. "I was also complimenting him on his promotion."

"I'd like to get to know him better. Think he might join us for a drink after we're finished?"

"I'll let you ask him, and if he agrees, don't include me. My guess would be you're interested in recruiting another member of Young Italy?"

"Charles, I liked it better when you claimed to be a naïve American," said Piero laughing as they joined their platoon for the opening formation of the troops.

At the end of the day, Piero did ask Ossoli to join him for a drink, and he accepted. At a nearby tratorria, drinks in hand, both relaxed and discussed the day's training until Piero mentioned he knew the Ossoli family had served the popes for generations.

"Yes, we have," said Ossoli, "and still do."

"And you'll continue the service?"

"No, my father and brothers do, but I'm the youngest and must chart my own course."

"Interesting. You should be proud of your family. Pio Nono is popular with the people."

"He is, but my interests lie elsewhere."

Piero took a sip of his wine and thought about what to say next. "I agree, the success of Pio Nono is obvious, but I'm interested in our Italian brothers and their campaigns to drive out the Austrians. I understand many of the cities in the north have established Civic Guards."

"They have. Someday we may all be fighting the Austrians together. That would be a great day for Italy," said Ossoli.

"This has been a pleasure, Lieutenant, I hope we can do it again," said Piero as they both rose to leave.

Piero went directly to Trastevere and the cameo workshop.

"What brings you here?" asked Donatangelo."

"I met someone today who may be of use to us. He's Lieutenant Ossoli, a member of the Ossli family close to the pope. Since his father and brothers are part of Pio Nono's government, I thought he might be a source of information useful for our activities."

"I'm aware of the family association with Pio Nono. I also have had one of our group watching Ossoli off and on because he was seen with Mazzini's friend, Margaret Fuller. It turns out he's more than a casual acquaintance of hers. We are convinced they are lovers."

"That's a surprise."

"It surprised me too, but that's none of our business. I'm not even going to ask Maria about it, because I'm certain she'll not want to talk about their relationship. Women are better at keeping secrets about such things than men."

"I get the feeling he's on our side."

"You may be right, but I don't want to interfere with Fuller's life. Mazzini was emphatic that we are to give her all the assistance she needs, nothing else," said Donatangelo. "I have no problem with you and Ossoli being friends, but you should not make any attempt to recruit him for Young Italy."

⸻

After Margaret left Rome, Ossoli became a frequent visitor to the studio, checking every day to see if a letter from her had arrived. He made no attempt to disguise his loneliness, but that didn't bother Charles, who enjoyed his company. Piero would sometimes join them at the Caffé Greco, where, once his artist friends discovered Ossoli had a title, he became a celebrity.

The talk at the café always turned to politics and Pio Nono. Ossoli listened but said little. He couldn't understand why these young artists, immersed in the beauty of painting or sculpture, always preferred to talk of revolution. Leaving the café one night, he said to Charles, "Do these artists have nothing else to discuss or is talk of revolution part of their training?"

Charles thought before answering, "You know, I'm so accustomed to hearing about politics in the café, I never thought about it. You're right, they are boring. Perhaps it's because artists are always looking for new ideas, something different, and politics is all about making rules controlling everyone's behavior. They feel they need an atmosphere of complete freedom to create unique work. Or they cannot sell their work and have no money. In that case they can always blame the government for their failure. But you're right, you would think it was a requirement for being an artist."

After four weeks, the letter Ossoli was hoping for arrived. Margaret was cutting her trip short and would be home two weeks earlier than planned. He was ecstatic and after he left the studio, Maria said, "Seems they're both lonely." Charles nodded in agreement.

Margaret's return would also resolve Maria's boredom. She missed her and the excitement she generated. What she missed most of all was her conversations about the role of women in society, both in Italy and America

Early in December Maria noticed Margaret appeared preoccupied and, at times. distracted. Then, at the end of one of their busier days Margaret asked her to stay and have coffee.

As she prepared the coffee Maria said, "Are you all right? You seem to have less energy since you returned to Rome."

"Women notice these little things, don't they?'" said Margaret as she poured the coffee. "I should be happy. Christmas is coming and it's my favorite time of year, but this Christmas is going to be different from all the others in my life. Maria, I need your advice."

"Of course. What can I do?"

"I'm almost certain I'm with child."

"*O Dio mio!*" exclaimed Maria. "Have you told Ossoli?"

"Not yet. First, I want to be certain. Can you find me a good doctor?"

"I know a good one nearby who can be trusted. I'll make an appointment tomorrow."

"This would come as a great shock to my family and friends. I never thought I'd find myself in this situation. I've been thinking about it for days and have some ideas, but need your advice. I probably can continue working for at least another four months before I can no longer hide my condition."

"I think you can. At least four months for certain."

"Then I want to leave Rome for the last months, but still want to be close enough for Ossoli to visit me."

"How do you think he'll react when you tell him you're going to have a baby?"

"I think he'll be thrilled. He wants desperately to get married and this would be the best reason. He'll be happy."

"And you. Would you get married?"

"I've not decided."

"Will you be returning to Rome after the delivery?"

"Yes, but I'd like to leave the baby behind to be nursed."

"You're not abandoning the baby, are you?"

"No, I want this baby and that's another thing I need you to do. Find me a place close to Rome where I can make all this happen. Can you do that?"

"I've never done anything like that, but I have friends where I used to live who come from different villages near Rome. They'll help me."

"This may be too early to make plans, but it's all I think about now," said Margaret.

Maria assured her, "When it comes time to for you to leave the city I'll help you get settled."

"Thank you," said Margaret. "You've been such a dear friend. I know I can depend on you during the difficult time ahead. You're my Italian treasure."

The next day the doctor confirmed her condition. Now, Margaret had to tell Giovanni. She spent all day rehearsing what she would say, but when he arrived in the evening and placed his arms around her, drew her close, and kissed her she withdrew quickly. It was obvious to him something was wrong.

"That's not the Margaret I know," said Giovanni. "What's wrong?"

She turned away, then looked back at him and said with obvious anguish in her voice, "I have to tell you something. Let's sit down."

He didn't know what to expect because she had never acted this way before and could only think the worse. He waited for her to speak.

"I went to see a doctor today and he confirmed what I suspected—I'm going to have a baby."

He jumped up and shouted, "Fantastic. What good news." He reached down and pulled Margaret to her feet and kissed her, but her response remained muted.

"Why aren't you happy? This is wonderful. Are you trying to tell me you don't want the baby?"

Still in his arms she said, "I want the baby, but my family and friends have no idea about you, and I have no idea how to tell them."

"We must be married as soon as possible."

"No, I have to think about this."

"What is there to think about? We're in love. We're going to have a child. We must get married for the sake of the child."

"I love you, Giovanni. That hasn't changed. But having a child will change my life. I need time to think."

Looking disappointed and confused he said, "I know you love me but I cannot understand why you will not marry me. My love for you will not change. I'll never leave your side."

It was difficult to find a place outside Rome where Margaret could stay until the birth of her child, but Maria finally met an interested couple from Rieti, sixty kilometers northeast of Rome. Margaret interviewed the woman who also agreed to nurse and care for the baby when she returned to Rome to resume her work.

This was disturbing to Maria who could not imagine leaving your child with a wet nurse and going on with their life as though nothing ever happened. She yearned to have a child and knew she could never leave it to be cared for by another woman. Not ever.

CHAPTER EIGHT

Assassination

Charles was accustomed to exchanging gifts on Christmas morning instead of the Feast of Epiphany as they did in in Italy. When Maria awoke Christmas morning she found a neatly wrapped package on her bedside stand. Still half asleep she sat staring at it until Charles said *"Buon Natale.* Go ahead open it."

Inside, in a tiny felt-lined box was a diamond ring. This surprise brought tears to her eyes, not only because she loved her husband and found the ring beautiful, but for her it was symbolic of the transition the two were making from impoverished lovers to people of means. His blossoming career had changed both their lives. Before she met Charles, she would never have imagined having something so elegant. She didn't need an expensive present to appreciate another Christmas with him. The haunting wounds of her past were healing.

Returning from a meeting of Young Italy during the week after Christmas Maria announced to Charles, "I want us both to participate in a demonstration on New Year's Day."

"I assume this has something to do with Young Italy?" he asked.

"Yes, but all we have to do is be part of the crowd."

"Will you be involved?"

"No."

"What's this all about?"

"Mazzini thinks it's time to increase the pressure on Pio Nono to join the struggle against the Austrians. He thinks it's only a matter of time before a revolution breaks out in France and after that, Prussia. Why not change in Italy in 1848?"

"You promise me we only have to be part of the crowd?"

"I promise," Maria assured him.

On New Year's Day they arrived at the Piazza del Quirinale about noon. Entering the piazza, they paused to scan the broad space with the tall obelisk and fountain dominating its center. A large crowd had gathered before the Quirinal. Above its massive door was the balcony, flanked by the Papal flag on the right and the flag of the Papal States on the left. Pio Nono used this balcony to address or bless his people on special occasions. The mere size of the building was meant to be a symbol of power.

They noticed a disturbance at the opposite end of the Piazza. Maria tugged at Charles's arm pulling him toward it. As they approached they could hear a man shouting to the crowd. He was preaching, but preaching politics, and many in the crowd were nodding in agreement or encouraging his polemic with shouts of, "*Sì, Sì.*"

Soon other speakers could be heard throughout the piazza, haranguing the people with their tirades about the lack of initiative Pio Nono had shown in joining those in the north fighting the Austrians. As they moved from group to group the constant theme of unification of the Italian peninsula made it clear to Charles he was witnessing a planned agitation of the people to extoll the credo of Young Italy and the other secret societies and liberals of Rome.

He watched Maria who seemed to be mesmerized by the speakers and realized he felt a little jealous of her involvement with Young

Italy. That look on her face frightened him. The world of politics never interested him. She had introduced him to the beauty of love and changed his life. He was an American citizen with an Italian wife. Could love trump patriotism? As far as he was concerned, it must, and he would stop at nothing to make certain it did.

Then there was a sudden rush of people to the center of the piazza. She grabbed his hand and he almost stumbled as they ran to see what was happening. To his surprise, he saw Piero climbing to the base of the obelisk. From his perch, he began speaking to the crowd, "Why do we stand by and do nothing while our brothers in the north shed their blood fighting the Austrians? This is also our fight, but Pio Nono refuses to accept his responsibility in this struggle for the soul of Italy. Only one solution is possible to this invasion of our beloved land by the Austrians—driving out the intruders and unifying Italy."

Charles had no idea Piero was such a good speaker. No question he had the people's attention and sympathy. After he had been speaking for about thirty minutes and the emotions of the crowd seemed to be peaking, he jumped down to the piazza and led them toward the door of the Quirinal. He and several of his followers began pounding on the door demanding Pio Nono come out and address the crowd.

Charles had to admire how organized this supposedly spontaneous demonstration appeared. Of course, the door to the Quirinal did not open, but the pounding and the crowd shouting encouragement louder and louder, could not be ignored inside. They expected Pio Nono to come onto the balcony to reject the claims of the speakers. But he did not.

After about two hours of continuous demonstrations word spread that Pio Nono was coming out, but instead of appearing on the balcony to address the crowd, his carriage exited the rear of the Quirinal and headed for the piazza. The closer it came to the piazza the quieter the demonstrators became.

When he reached the edge of the piazza Pio Nono's strongest advocate and man of the people, Ciceruacchio, jumped on the back of the carriage waving the flag of the Papal States. As the carriage made its way around the piazza Pio Nono blessed the crowd and Ciceruacchio shouted, *"Corragio Santo Padre, Corragio Santo Padre."* The appearance of Pio Nono with his popular supporter transformed the mood of the people and by the time the carriage had completed a circle of the piazza the people began to disperse. Charles concluded it was a draw.

The events in Rome provided Margaret Fuller with more than enough material to send a dispatch to New York every week. She needed the money to pay for her upcoming confinement.

In February 1848, the monarchy of King Louis Philippe was overthrown by the people of Paris establishing the Second Republic of France which championed the right to work for all citizens. Karl Marx published his *Manifesto of the Communist Party* in March. Uprisings were occurring in southern Italy and successful campaigns against the Austrians in Milan and Venice ignited a renewed spirit of revolution in the north. After the successes in Milan, Mazzini returned to Italy in April 1848, fourteen years after having been banned from the country. Political unrest had indeed become the theme for the year 1848.

Margaret found her pregnancy increasingly difficult to conceal. Reluctant to leave Rome and interrupt her reporting during these exciting times she decided she had no choice if she wished to keep her pregnancy private. It was time to go to Rieti.

Ossoli and Maria would be accompanying her on the trip and Maria convinced Charles to join them. He had been working constantly on his commissions and she felt he needed a vacation. Neither had been away from Rome since their adventure in Civitavecchia. It took some convincing to get him away from the studio, but he agreed on the condition they return in four days.

The group left Rome in late May for the five-hour carriage ride to Rieti. It was a perfect time to travel, but Margaret looked sad and said little during the trip. The fresh spring air, blossoming trees along the roadside, and a clear sky improved everyone's spirits except Margaret's. Rieti, a city of about fifty thousand, was set in a beautiful valley surrounded by the Sabatini and Rietini mountains.

Once they had settled Margaret in her temporary apartment Maria packed a lunch and she and Charles set off to explore one of the many trails leading into the foothills surrounding Rieti. He had never taken an all-day hike, but for her it was a reminder of her days in her mountain village.

When they reached a small lake, they found a secluded spot for lunch. The beauty of the forest, the fresh air, and the peaceful surroundings relaxed Charles. After finishing their lunch and a bottle of wine they dozed in each other's arms.

He woke first, and inspired by the idyllic setting, woke Maria with a kiss. Her passionate response made it clear she wished for more and the two spent the next hour immersed in their special world of love. Fulfilled and happy, neither said anything for the longest time.

He broke the silence with, "Thanks for making me come with you. I needed this. I've been too involved with my work. We must do this more often."

"Which, come to Rieti or make love?" Maria chuckled.

"You know what I mean."

"I do. We both have become too involved with work. We can afford to enjoy other things in life."

"Now I wish we could stay longer."

"It would be nice, but it's time to leave Margaret and Ossoli alone. They have a lot to do and we would be in the way. Ossoli wants nothing more than to take care of Margaret. I heard you two discussing the Civic Guard again. What was that all about?"

"Things have changed in the past month. Many in our regiment were activated to accompany the Papal troops on their recent deployment to the northern part of the province. Why I wasn't chosen to join them is a mystery."

"Thank God you weren't. I'm concerned. Donatangelo is convinced we are close to a revolution in Rome."

"Everett Brown's family told him to leave Rome or they'll stop sending him money. They want him back in America. Margaret's dispatches about the unrest here and in France must be having an effect in America".

"How can he leave if he's a member of the Civic Guard?"

"He'll find a way. He may already be gone."

"Do you want to leave Rome?"

"No. I have the commissions to complete, and that's a lot of money for us. And this is our home. For now, I think we should stay, but I want to take you to America to meet my parents. Perhaps next year."

"And your service with the Civic Guard will continue?"

"As I said, this is our home. I love it here. Up until now they've avoided putting their expatriate troops in any dangerous situations. Let's hope they continue to do so."

"But if Donatangelo's right, and if there is a revolution the Civic Guard will have to become involved."

"You know I avoid discussing these things, but I do listen to your comments after you've attended a Young Italy meeting. And I read the newspapers, but the scariest things I hear are at the Caffé Greco where artists from all over the world speak only of revolution. It has happened in France and now Prussia. No question in their minds we're next."

"Oh, my love, I'm so happy, yet it never occurred to me I would end up in this quandary of risking my happiness for a cause," said Maria. "What have I done?"

"You've made an American happier than he believed possible, that's what you've done," said Charles. "We'll get through this."

⸻

"Thank you for coming Piero," said Donatangelo.

"The message sounded urgent," said Piero.

"Sorry, not an emergency, but I'm excited. I received an interesting communique from Mazzini regarding Pio Nono's tepid response to the Austrian invasion of the northern border of the Papal States and occupation of Ferrara."

"I've been following that in the newspapers. The resignation of Pio Nono's chief minister, in protest over Pio Nono's inaction, makes it even worse for him. It's a major topic of conversation on the streets."

"And today, I heard Pio Nono has decided to replace his previous minister with Pellegrino Rossi, a conservative and favorite of the cardinals. Mazzini thinks it's time for action. The people are disillusioned and Pio Nono's popularity is decreasing.

"The other news is that Garibaldi has returned to Italy with sixty of his best men. Mazzini has been told Garibaldi offered his services to Pio Nono. He rejected the offer. Garibaldi is already recruiting men to fight the Austrians. Mazzini plans to meet with him and try to convince him to move his growing army closer to Rome."

"I heard Pio Nono's greatest supporter, Ciceruacchio, has lost confidence in the pope. That's a major change," said Piero.

"I also heard that and think it's time for us to meet with him,' said Donatangelo.

Piero was surprised at how quickly Ciceruacchio agreed to meet Donatangelo. When he arrived at the cameo workshop, the two paused, as they took the measure of each other. Donatangelo broke the silence with, "Thank you for coming. I've wanted to meet with you for a long time. I've followed your skillful support of Pio Nono. You are a powerful advocate for your beliefs and have the confidence of the people, but I understand you have become disenchanted with the pope."

"Disenchanted is too weak a word," said Ciceruacchio. "And by the way, you can call me Angelo, Angelo Brunetti, my given name.

Our people are dying in the north. The Austrians are having their way and Pio Nono allows it to continue. He wants to remain the temporal leader of the Papal States and at the same time spiritual head of the Catholic Church. He can no longer have it both ways."

"Exactly our feeling," said Donatangelo.

"You have used "we" and "our". Who are you speaking for?" asked Brunetti.

"I think we can trust you now. Young Italy, and I'm certain the other secret societies, the Circolo di Roma, feel the same way."

"And you're in touch with Mazzini, the father of this group everyone in Rome knows exists?"

"Yes, we are. He's our inspiration and has never wavered in his belief in a unified Italy. And, I sense, neither have you. We would like you to join our movement or at least support it. All these recent uprisings throughout Italy are coming to a head and we're prepared to openly join the struggle for which so many of our fellow Italians have fought and died," said Donatangelo. "It's time for an uprising in Rome."

"Strong words. I agree, but we have no guns or cannons. Words alone will not do the job."

"We do have arms. We've been stockpiling guns and ammunition for the past year. How do you think the Civic Guard will react if there is an uprising of the people?"

"An interesting question. I've been thinking of the same thing. If they see the uprising is organized, I feel they'll support it."

"So, do we. We feel the time has come," said Donatangelo.

"I agree, but we need a major incident. Something dramatic and unexpected that will ignite the people's desire for change. I have a sense of how people can be manipulated, but here we are not talking of swaying opinion. We are talking about instigating a revolution. Let me think about it," said Brunetti.

"Thank you, my friend. I'll inform the others in our society and the Circolo di Roma about this meeting," said Donatangelo. "By the way, I'm sure you're aware Garibaldi has returned to Italy?"

"I am," said Brunetti. "Perhaps we can convince him to join our revolution."

Charles and Maria were having dinner when someone began banging on the apartment door. When he opened it a jubilant Ossoli threw his arms around him and shouted over and over, "I'm a father, I'm a father!"

Maria rushed over to hug him and asked, "A boy or a girl?"

"A boy. I have a son."

"When did this happen?" asked Charles.

"Yesterday, September 5th. And Margaret is doing fine," said Ossoli. "I had to let you know tonight because I'm leaving for Rieti early in the morning. We have Civic Guard training tomorrow. Would you explain to our commander why I'm not present? He'll understand."

"I'll be glad to. I'm sure he will. Give our congratulations to Margaret," said Charles. Without another word, Ossoli turned and left running down the stairs. Charles and Maria, laughed.

Margaret was indeed doing fine. Motherhood gave her a sense of joy beyond anything she had experienced before. For a time, she forgot about writing and politics. All her attention was devoted to Nino, as she called him.

They were a happy family until Giovanni announced, "It is time for our son's baptism. We must make plans now, so I can let my superiors in the Civic Guard know when I'll be away."

This caught Margaret by surprise. Her son would be baptized a Roman Catholic. She was a follower of the Transcendentalist movement which was opposed to many Catholic beliefs. But there were no other options in Rieti. "Can't we wait until we're back in Rome?" said Margaret hoping to check his enthusiasm.

"In Italy it's traditional to baptize a baby in the first six weeks. It's an important ceremony, one not to be delayed. We must get married."

Flustered by Giovanni's determined attitude, all she could think to say was, "Right now? This is all happening too fast."

"The child cannot be baptized with two names. I want my son's name registered in the records of the cathedral, here in Rieti. Ossoli is a noble name, and I'm the proud father. Nino must begin his life with his parents registered as the Marchese and Marchesa Ossoli. I love you with all my heart and now I beg you to become my wife."

Margaret paced back and forth considering what he had said before answering, "You've brought a happiness to my life I never knew existed and this beautiful child. You're right. It's time. I'll marry you."

Because of the long history of the Ossoli family's service to the papacy, Giovanni was able to expedite a private marriage service and the baptism of Angelo Eugenio Filippo Ossoli a month later.

On his return to Rome, Ossoli asked Maria to find a smaller apartment for Margaret. They had agreed it would be best to leave Nino with the wet-nurse in Rieti giving Margaret time to concentrate on her writing. She needed the money. Once again, Maria could not imagine such a separation of a mother and child, but did as asked and found her a small apartment overlooking the Piazza Barberini.

Ciceruacchio contacted Donatangelo the first week in November asking him to arrange a meeting with the leaders of the other secret groups in Rome. Ciceruacchio told them he had a plan he felt would challenge Pio Nono's government and incite the people to demand he respond to their disenchantment with his leadership.

He did not tell them exactly what would happen, only said it would occur the morning of the opening of the Chamber of Deputies, November 15. He wanted the secret societies to organize a demonstration in the piazza outside the Chamber building to protest the inaction of Pio Nono to the intrusion of the Austrians into the Papal State. They all agreed.

Keeping this plan secret was impossible with so many people involved. The papal government intelligence service alerted to the plan, stationed Carbineers in the piazza. They also activated Charles's Civic Guard unit to patrol the streets of the surrounding area. They were not armed.

Despite the cloudy cold morning of November 15, people filled the piazza. Carbineers, with their carbines lined its perimeter. The crowd shouted their support of the inflammatory taunts of the agitators directed at the deputies and Pio Nono. As members of Young Italy galvanized the people into a frenzy, Maria looked for Donatangelo and didn't see him. But she was convinced he was there, lurking somewhere in the background.

Ossoli and his men were to patrol a street about fifty meters from the piazza. They could hear the shouts of the crowd, but could not see into the piazza. All this confused Charles. If they were expecting trouble why were the Civic Guard not armed? They had taken their position early in the morning and watched the armed Carbineers march into the piazza. He became concerned. Maria was in the crowd.

Pio Nono's chief minister, Pellegrino Rossi, who was to address the opening of Chamber of Deputies, arrived fifteen minutes late. When his carriage entered the piazza, the angry crowd recognized it was Rossi, a man disliked by almost all Romans except the conservatives, and began jeering and shouting all sorts of demeaning epithets at him. Once the carriage stopped they pushed forward and encircled it, making it difficult for Rossi to exit. When he did, he made it clear he was not intimidated and responded to the crowd with a look of defiance.

As Rossi made his way to the entrance a group of four men pushed through the crowd moving toward him. Suddenly, as Rossi reached the first steps of the building, one of the four men lunged forward, knife in hand, and stabbed him in the neck.

Rossi collapsed to the pavement grasping at the wound gushing blood from his severed carotid artery. Screams erupted throughout the piazza, but no one rushed to help him. He died within minutes.

Nor was any attempt made by the crowd or Carbineers to seize the assassin or his accomplices. A cloak was thrown over the assassin's head by one of the coconspirators and the crowd parted, allowing them to leave the piazza unobstructed. It was all over in less than five minutes. Finally, two men came down from the building and dragged Rossi's body into the chamber. In shocked disbelief silence came over the crowd, but it was brief. The agitators began to remind them the dead man had represented everything they disliked about Pio Nono's government.

When people came running from the direction of the piazza shouting, "They killed him, they killed him, he's dead," it panicked Charles, who had no idea who they meant. He wanted to run to the piazza to look for Maria. Ossoli told his men they should return to headquarters to get their muskets, but their commander came down the street on horseback and told the men, "No shots have been fired. Stay where you are. Rossi has been assassinated."

After another ten minutes the crowd in the piazza began to disperse. Charles watched for Maria but didn't see her. He became worried, but the Civic Guard was told to remain in position until dark. He couldn't understand why. Once the piazza emptied the street was quiet and time passed painfully slow. An uneasy calm settled over the streets of Rome.

When the Civic Guard were finally released from duty, they were told to report for duty the next morning. No explanation was given. Charles rushed home, ran up the stairs to the apartment. When he saw Maria was safe he threw his arms around and held her tight. "I was worried about you. What happened?"

"I thought we would be protesting like we did on New Year's Day. It began that way, but then it changed quickly. Rossi was stabbed in the neck and bled to death in minutes on the steps of the Chamber building. It was brutal."

"And it happened in front of a thousand witnesses, including a company of Carbineers and nobody seized the assassin?"

"The assassin and his helpers left untouched."

"That's so Italian, so Roman. A thousand witnesses temporarily blind to an assassination occurring before their eyes. Thank goodness no shots were fired by the Carbineers. If something like this can happen with the complicity of so many people I think we've witnessed the beginning of a much broader conspiracy to bring down the government of Pio Nono."

Maria didn't react to his comment but said, "I met Donatangelo on my way home, and he said there's going to be another demonstration tomorrow. They're planning a parade from the Piazza del Popolo to the Chamber of Deputies."

"We were told to report to duty tomorrow morning. That must be the reason. I hope you're not planning on going. Two demonstrations in two days. That has to concern Pio Nono and his conservative cardinals. They may decide to disrupt this parade with force. Why do you have to go? It could become dangerous."

"Remember, I'm a member of Young Italy. We want change and this is an important time. It's only a parade."

"Remember. How can I forget? I want you to stay home," demanded Charles. He had never spoken to her that way.

"I'm not staying home," she replied, calmly, but in a tone that made it clear she was not about to change her mind.

He had no idea how to respond and did his best to control his dismay. He turned and began to walk away, but then turned back and said angrily, "We've discussed this before. You said you would avoid any dangerous activity with Young Italy. I'm concerned this parade may become violent. I don't want you to be part of it."

"The parade won't be dangerous. I'm not going to change my mind. I'm going," said Maria matching his angry tone. Then, she turned and walked to their bedroom.

Tired and overruled by his wife for the first time in their marriage, he was not about to follow her into the bedroom. He was too proud to do that. He went into their sitting room, stretched out on the sofa, and considered what had occurred between them. Was Maria in love with him or Young Italy? He was only trying to protect her.

Something dramatic had happened in Rome today. This was not the city he found when he first arrived to study with Morretti. A precarious political transformation was unfolding. It had already been the cause for tonight's quarrel. The fear of losing Maria once again terrified him. It took a long time, but eventually he fell asleep.

The next morning, Charles overslept and when he went into the bedroom looking for Maria, but she was already gone. A feeling of helplessness overwhelmed him. His immediate reaction was to run to the Piazza del Popolo and try to find her, but he knew that would be futile. If yesterday's crowd was any indication of the size of today's demonstration, it would probably be larger, and he would have little chance of finding her. He wished he had swallowed his pride and followed her into the bedroom last night.

He quickly put on his uniform, stopped for a quick cup of espresso, and ran to join his platoon. Ossoli was waiting for him and handed him his musket. He said they were going to the Piazza del Popolo to patrol a parade being organized to march to the Chamber of Deputies.

When they reached the piazza and he saw the police and Carbineers would also be marching, his fears were confirmed. The police and Carbineers were supposed to protect the pope, not march in a parade challenging his leadership. This was a revolution in the making. A marching band was set to lead the parade. Only in Italy, he thought.

The band struck up, a great cheer rose from the demonstrators, and the march began. The streets were lined with people cheering them on, waving banners, and sometimes sheets or towels, from their windows. The look of pride on the men marching was obvious, but the jubilation was lost on him. He could only think of his wife.

When they arrived at the Chamber of Deputies they were met by a deputy who was sent to explain what would be required to form a new ministry after Rossi's assassination. It was a typical boring bureaucratic description which did more to further upset the crowd than pacify it. Most couldn't hear him anyway.

The agitators of the Circolo di Roma shouted down the deputy who quickly recognized it would be best for him to return to the Chamber immediately. Shouts of, "*E abbastanza*" or "It's enough," came from the demonstrators who were told by the agitators to move on to the Quirinal. As they walked past, Charles noticed there were men in the crowd armed with pistols. Maria was nowhere in sight.

When they arrived at the Piazza di Quirinale, Pio Nono's response was to send one of his cardinals to address the demonstrators and assure them a new cabinet would be formed. This feeble response by Pio Nono to the dramatic events of the past two days did little to placate the protesters who shouted their disapproval. They wanted Pio Nono to agree to send troops to fight the Austrians. And now.

Ossoli's platoon, , was in the front line of the formation of Civic Guards in the piazza with angry protesters on either side. Charles watched the armed Swiss guards positioned in windows of the Quirinal. They looked uneasy and as the shouting became louder and more threatening, two guards fired into the crowd hitting two demonstrators. Pistol fire was returned from the angry crowd and panic ensued.

People fled from the piazza tripping over one another in the chaos of the stampeding crowd. Charles realized if the Swiss Guards fired again from the palace, he would be an easy target and, worse, he would be told to return fire.

That would be combat. Far from the reality of an actual battle, but nonetheless, the purpose would be to kill. Could he shoot someone? He was about to find out and there was no time to mentally debate the issue. If he reacted it would be by instinct. Wasn't that how they trained soldiers—if you are fired at, fire back? At least that would be his justification for killing someone. And still no sight of Maria.

When thirty minutes passed and there was no further response from Pio Nono, the remaining demonstrators became unruly. Suddenly another shot was fired. Someone in his platoon had fired his musket. The troops behind, as inexperienced and nervous as the men in the front line, assumed the Swiss Guards were again firing at the crowd and instinctively returned fire. He was about to fire when he heard Ossoli shouting "Hold your fire, hold your fire! It was an accident."

The gunfire panicked the remaining protesters. Women screamed, but this time the screams coming from the opposite end of the piazza had a hideous agonizing sound. He could see the lifeless bodies of a man and woman being carried from the piazza. They were too far for him to get a good look at the woman. His heart began to race and he wanted to run from the piazza to see if it was Maria, but Piero grabbed him by the arm and said, "I know what you're thinking. That wasn't Maria. I could see, it was an older woman."

The better trained and disciplined Carbineers surrounding the piazza did not fire because no command had been given. The indiscriminate shots from the skittish Civic Guard fortunately hadn't hit anyone. The only victim was the stone facade of the Quirinal. The shooting prompted Pio Nono to dismiss the Swiss Guards and send another cardinal to reiterate his promise to form a new ministry immediately. But he still gave no indication he was going to send troops to fight the Austrians as the crowd demanded. Weary from the day's unsuccessful demonstrations, the crowd began to disperse.

On his way home Charles decided the only thing about him resembling a soldier was his uniform and musket. Now he understood why training and discipline, no matter how repetitive and boring were essential to success and survival. His first test under fire, not even hostile fire, had been a failure. Belonging to the Civic Guard was no longer a simple diversion and he had no idea how to deal with either it or Maria.

When he reached the apartment he hesitated before opening the door. What should he say? When he walked in he couldn't have been more surprised. A subdued Maria said, "Thank God you're safe. It was crazy in the piazza." It was a though nothing had happened last night.

"You left this morning without even saying good bye. Why?" asked a bewildered Charles. "I don't understand what I did wrong. I only wanted to protect you." She walked over, put her arms around him and held him tight.

Still holding him close, she looked up and said, "You're so different from the men in Italy. When a woman disobeyed her husband in my village, they would be beaten. I was as confused as you when you didn't yell at me or even show any sign of anger. I think I saw it as a sign of weakness. How stupid of me.

"In two days, I've seen three people killed. You were right about the possibility of the march becoming dangerous. That made me begin to think about last night. I regret what I did. Then I was afraid for you, and for those who decided to return to the piazza. I'm beginning to understand not only how much you love me, but how much you respect me. Respect from men was never a part of my life. I'll never do anything like that again. Please try to understand."

"I'll try," said Charles as he kissed her gently.

"What happened? I fled after the Swiss Guards shot into the crowd. As I was running from the piazza I heard more shots. Were more people killed?"

"It was all a stupid mistake. One of our men fired accidentally. Then those behind our line fired without thinking. We were lucky no one else was killed. Ossoli prevented any further shooting in the ranks and when Pio Nono dismissed the Swiss Guards, the demonstrators left."

"What will tomorrow bring?"

"I doubt your Young Italy friends will discontinue their challenge of the government. At the moment, they have the advantage. I'm surprised the streets are calm."

"Do you have to report for duty again tomorrow?"

"Yes. I need to get back to the studio and see what my carvers have done, but I'm not sure when I can. I want you to see if they've made any progress," said Charles. "I'm tired and need some sleep."

"I went there earlier and they weren't working. They were probably part of the demonstration. I'll check again tomorrow," said Maria.

CHAPTER NINE

An Unexpected Outcome

C ontrary to what many expected, Rome remained tranquil. Pellegrino Rossi's assassination was a powerful message to Pio Nono. The undercurrent of protest in the city did not abate, despite Pio Nono's appointment of a new minister and attempts to restructure his government.

During the night of November 24, disguised as a priest, Pio Nono fled Rome. People were shocked by the news. His whereabouts were unknown. It was rumored he had boarded a ship in Civitavecchia and another rumor had him still in the Papal States in San Felice. In the weeks before Pio Nono fled, he had appointed a group of influential Romans to a council, *The National Popular Club of Rome.* They were to support the actions of the Chamber of Deputies and act as a stabilizing force. The council published a proclamation in the Roman newspapers:

The PONTIFF has left Rome. Before his departure he confirmed the present ministry by a paper in his own handwriting, recommending to their care the public order and the preservation of property amongst all classes.

The ministry, therefore, in the fullness of their power, will not turn back from the path they have entered: they trust that the people of Rome, generously pardoning those who would fain [sic] to bring on a civil war, will scrupulously avoid every act tending to disaster. Let all the military, civil and legislative authorities unite their efforts so that Rome, an example of civilization to all nations, may shew [sic] her enemies that, in the midst of the most trying circumstances, she knows how to preserve the profoundest tranquility and the most conscientious respect for human laws.

The Civic Guard, initiated for the maintenance of order and constitutional freedom, will suffice together with the valorous troops of the line, to save their country a second time from any attempt against its quiet.

Viva Italia! Viva il Ministero democratio! Viva l'unione! November 25, 1848

Reading this, Charles knew the time he spent on duty with the Civic Guard would only increase or perhaps even take over his life. There was no way he could follow the example of Everett Brown and discretely leave Rome at this time. That would humiliate Maria, even though he knew she would follow him if he decided to return to America. His happiest years had been spent in Rome. His wife was Italian. For now, this was his life and his home. It was no time for regrets.

The streets of Rome may have been tranquil with Pio Nono gone, but the political situation was in disarray. Unaccustomed to making decisions without the pope's oversight, power struggles ensued. Each deputy had a solution or plan for the future and a strong leader was needed, but none emerged.

Pio Nono's location was finally disclosed. He was in Gaeta, a city south of Rome in the Kingdom of Naples. A steady flow of Roman clerics and diplomats descended on the city.

152

It took until February 1849 for the newly formed government to finalize their proposition for the future of Rome and the former Papal States. They issued the following proclamation:

Fundamental Decree

Art. 1. The Papacy has fallen in deed and right, from the temporal government of the Roman States.

Art. 2. The Roman Pontiff will have all the guarantees necessary for the independent exercise of spiritual power.

Art. 3. The form of government of the Roman States will be purely democratic and will take the glorious name of Roman Republic.

Art. 4. The Roman Republic will have those relations with the rest of Italy which the common nationality requires.

Charles was impressed by the brevity of these four articles that changed so much. Would itbe possible to end years of abuse of power by the papacy because of the brutal assassination of one minister? True, discontent pervaded the Papal States for years, but this was an overnight revolution involving no army or battle.

The result, four articles eliminating the temporal authority of a papacy embedded in the culture of a divided country and creation of a democracy in only one kingdom of Italy. This made Charles wonder if it was too dramatic a change at one time. The revolution in his own country, also ending the rule of a king, took years, many battles, and extensive loss of life. These contradictions left Charles uneasy.

The pope's influence extended beyond the borders of the Italy. It included the Catholic countries of France, Spain, and Austria, all having large armies. He could not believe Pio Nono would accept his loss of control over the Papal States.

Rome celebrated the news with possibly the largest parade since the time of ancient Rome. The city was decorated with banners and government representatives marched from their chamber to the Church of Ara-Coeli to celebrate a mass. Civic Guards lined the streets, but because of his expatriate status Charles was excused from duty.

Maria insisted he accompany her for the day's festivities. After Mass a large parade headed by the Carbineers and companies of the Civic Guard paraded through the decorated streets. They were followed by representatives of the various provinces waving their colorful local banners. For Maria this represented a stirring patriotic culmination to all she believed and the work she had done for Young Italy.

Charles admired the marchers for their pride and dignity, bordering on hubris, so characteristic of their culture. This was not a day for humility. Knowing all she had done to make this possible, he was pleased for Maria.

After the parade, celebrations continued throughout the city. Charles and Maria did not get home until after midnight. In bed she nudged him and said, "How can I possibly sleep tonight? All the excitement, the street parties, and the formation of a new democratic Republic. Is this how they celebrated the American Revolution?"

"I'm certain they celebrated, but how I don't know. For us it was a first. Italy has had such a long history of government changes. You've had a lot of practice," laughed Charles as he rolled away from her.

She gave him a good kick and said no more.

Mazzini retuned to a hero's welcome on March 8, 1849. The new government had already proclaimed him a citizen of Rome in absentia. Maria burst into the studio the next day and almost knocked Charles down as he worked, shouting, "I met him, I met him."

"Who did you meet? Who made you this excited?"

"Mazzini. He came to visit Margaret and she introduced me to him. I was speechless. He was so nice and polite. A gentleman."

"A gentleman with powerful ideas that may have toppled Pio Nono from his throne. I'm impressed Mazzini would visit her so soon after his arrival in Rome. I hadn't heard he was here. What did they talk about?"

"Margaret dismissed me, but meeting the great man, the founder of Young Italy, was special. I can't wait to tell Donatangelo and Piero."

"All the talk in the trattorias has been about this man Garibaldi, or General Garibaldi as they call him," said Charles. "He's also in Rome and has an army of a thousand men camped outside Rieti. They claim he's the one warrior who can protect Rome and lead Italy to unification.

"Now we also have the great intellectual leader Mazzini in Rome. I don't pretend to be an expert on the intricacies of Roman politics, but the presence in Rome of these two powerful men must be concerning to Pio Nono and his Catholic followers on the Continent."

"What do you mean?"

"I mean Pio Nono will not remain in Gaeta," said Charles. "The papacy and Rome are immutable. It's obvious he cannot depend on support from his former Papal States or anywhere else in Italy. He'll have to look elsewhere, and that would be the Catholic countries on the Continent."

"You think there'll be fighting?"

"I hope not, but with these two interlopers in Rome, it may be the only way Pio Nono has any chance to return."

———

Indeed, Pio Nono had already sent emissaries to France and Spain asking them to send troops to occupy Rome. At least that was how the French interpreted the request. The French General Oudinot arrived in Civitavecchia with eight thousand troops in late April. His orders from the French president, Louis-Napoleon Bonaparte were to march into Rome and secure the city for the return of Pio Nono. Force was to be employed only if necessary, because the French were convinced the Italians would not fight.

Two days later, Garibaldi led his troops from Rieti into Rome. As this charismatic general paraded through the streets with his loyal cadre of redshirts and volunteers, both the young and old were energized to defend their city and the new republic. The most enthusiastic of the volunteers were the numerous young artists of Rome. Enough volunteered to form their own company armed with the guns and ammunition supplied by Young Italy. Contrary to the French intelligence provided by the clerics in Rome, the Italians were ready to fight.

The entire Civic Guard was activated and city prepared for war. The papal troops, now sympathetic to the people, and Carbineers joined General Garibaldi. With all the volunteers joining the defense of the city Rome was prepared to meet the French troops with an army of about nine thousand. Trees were cut down to construct barricades on the streets leading from the gates on the east side of the city.

Charles was in his studio when he heard the unsettling beat of the drums used to alert the Civic Guard for immediate duty. His inclination was to continue working and finish the day, but all his carvers and staff stopped whatever they were doing and excused themselves, saying they needed to join the rest of the city preparing for war. His worst fears had materialized.

As he was changing into his Civic Guard uniform, Maria came running into their apartment shouting, "Charles, Charles, I was with Margaret and Ossoli when I heard the drums. Everything is happening so fast."

"Did Ossoli leave?"

"Yes, immediately. I'm afraid. There are so many rumors on the streets. People are saying there are fifteen thousand French troops coming from Civitavecchia, others say twenty thousand. I don't know what to believe."

"I think it's safe to say the French troops are on their way, how many we'll soon find out. I'm concerned about your safety while I'm away."

"I won't be alone. I'll be with Margaret. Mazzini has appointed her head of the hospital being organized on Tiber Island to handle the casualties. I'll be spending all my time assisting her there."

"Good, that makes me feel a little better. I don't want you on the streets at a time like this. Stay at the hospital and sleep there. It'll be safer. Let's lock up and I'll walk you back to Margaret's before I join the Civic Guard."

Reaching Margaret's apartment on the Piazza Barberini was not easy. The streets were filled with people making frantic preparations for the expected battle. The food shops were empty and women were carrying large jugs of water on their heads. Preparing for the worst, windows were being shuttered everywhere creating an odd staccato sound of wood striking stone in the narrow streets.

All this increased Charles's apprehension. At the moment, all he knew was an army was approaching Rome and he could be fighting for the defense of his adopted home, but even scarier, for his life. Would he ever see Maria again?

When they reached Margaret's apartment it was time to say good-bye. They embraced with frenzied passion. Maria cried. All she could say over and over was, "Be careful my love, be careful, be careful. I'll be waiting at the hospital."

At the headquarters of the Civic Guard, there were more troops than he had ever seen at one time milling about with officers shouting and attempting to get them organized. The first problem was finding his company, but when he did, they had his musket ready for him. He was the last to arrive. After reporting to Ossolli he saw Smyth and Piero. "This may be the great adventure you wanted for your resume and biography," said Charles.

"It may be. Now I'm wondering if I'll survive. It would be a shame if I don't, because it sounds like this is going to be a big battle and it would look great in my biography," replied Smyth.

"We'll survive. It would be such a loss to the world of art if we don't," said Charles.

Laughing, Piero replied, "I think you both would agree, that's a bit of exaggeration."

Then the bugle sounded assembly and all the troops scrambled into their places. Ossoli ordered a roll call for his company and all were present except Everett Brown. As they stood at attention their commander, like Ossoli, a descendent of an aristocratic family wearing a finely tailored uniform, stood before the regiment. "Today," he began, "You will be facing a challenge for which we have trained over and over. Now it is time to implement this training in defense of our city. Part of the regiment will be held in reserve and part will be deployed along the city walls. God speed to you all."

Charles winced when he heard the words "we have trained over and over." The commander had obviously not been around, because Charles had no recollection of such training. He had been trained to patrol the streets and guard the gates. It didn't matter now though, they would have to go into battle and hope for the best. Perhaps, he would be part of the reserve force, but if the reserve force was needed, that would mean, the enemy was winning. He couldn't think of any good place to be with the Civic Guard today.

Ossoli put his men at ease and told them, "We're not going to be part of the reserve, we are to report to the Vatican wall near the old Porta Pertusa. Follow me. On the double. Move."

Charles was familiar with the gates of Rome. He had been on duty at most, but not the Porta Pertusa because it had been sealed. Why, he wondered are we going to defend a city gate sealed long ago?

On the double was a short-lived order. People, making their own last-minute preparations for a battle packed the narrow streets. Other troops heading in the same direction and barricades constructed with tree trunks and a mixture of old furniture and whatever was handy to fill any gaps, slowed their progress on the main thoroughfares.

At the Vatican wall, they were ordered to take a position on the rampart about twenty meters south of the old Porta Pertusa. Looking to this right and left Charles was impressed as he watched troops position themselves on the wide rampart.

Two cannons were about twenty meters to his right. But he still could not understand why they were defending a closed gate. With the troops settled on the rampart, Ossoli walked down the line telling the men, "No one is to fire unless I give the order. Check your bayonets to be sure they are firmly in place. Remember, watch me and listen to my commands. Our scouts tell us the French troops are headed for this side of the city. Where they will attack the wall is unknown. They are about two hours away."

The only good news was they still had time before they faced the French troops. Ossoli had set a rapid pace moving through Rome and climbing the narrow stairs to the rampart. Charles needed time to catch his breath. Resting with his back to the parapet he nudged Smyth on his left and said, "Can you believe this? We are about to fight a battle. Two foreign artists defending Rome."

"It's hard to imagine, let alone believe. Nor will anyone when I tell this story. They'll think I'm making it up. At home they know me as a bit of a coward when it comes to fights. Now I'm about to face thousands of French troops and there's no one from home to see this," said Smyth.

"The view from up here is spectacular," said Charles. "My guess would be we are at least ten meters high. It's a breathtaking sight."

"Perhaps when this is over I can come back and do a painting of Rome from here."

"Good idea," said Charles.

He looked around and noticed Piero dozing as an uncomfortable silence settled over the troops on the rampart of this massive wall. He also hoped they were in less danger here. Who would storm a gate no longer open? There were three other gates open, both south and north of their position.

Garibaldi was to defend the Janiculum, or high ground, on the west side of Rome overlooking Trastevere. If the French could capture this area, they would have a position above the walls and the perfect location from which to bombard the city with their batteries of cannons. He had twelve hundred troops led by his core of experienced redshirts.

Garibaldi did not place his troops on the city wall above Trastevere. Instead he deployed them outside the city wall around the Villa Corsini, surrounded by gardens, vineyards, and cornfields. The upper floor of the Villa Corsini was the high point of this position located near the Porta San Pancrazio, the gate where Garibaldi thought the French might attempt to make their entry into the city. Here, he was in a perfect position to watch their approach.

General Oudinot led only six thousand of his troops from Civitavecchia. His reports had led him to believe the Italians would not fight and that they would be welcomed to Rome. What he did not realize was his outdated maps failed to show the Porta Pertusa, where he planned to enter, was closed. It had been sealed with bricks and stones years ago.

In the old tower above the gate officers scanned the horizon with telescopes for any sight of the French troops. When they finally came into view the officers were dumbfounded. Oudonot was leading his troops straight toward Porta Pertusa. The troops on the rampart were alerted.

The alert was passed from man to man down the line. Ossoli, staying as low as possible told his men to prepare to fire, but stressed once again, only on his command. Charles, wishing this was all a bad dream, felt his heart pounding.

Having encountered no resistance on their approach to Rome, Oudinot was convinced the Italians were not prepared to fight and proceeded as planned marching his troops toward the Porta Pertusa.

The commander of the Civic Guard waited until the French were about fifty yards from the old gate and then gave the command for the two cannons to fire, followed by the command for the troops to fire. Ossoli shouted "Fire, fire." Charles, shocked by the blast of the cannons stood and fired, at what he had no idea. He looked to his left and saw Smyth frozen with fear. Ossoli came up from behind and shook Smyth, who at last began firing.

Ossoli moved back and forth encouraging his men. Reacting out of fear and panic, Charles continued to reload and fire. The combination of the blast of the cannons and the hundreds and hundreds of musket shots coming from both directions was deafening. This was a sound he would never forget. Smoke smelling of gunpowder settled on the rampart making it difficult to breathe.

Charles did not know how long he could endure. He saw two men hit by French fire fall. His instinct was to flee, but Ossoli, moving back and forth while firing his pistol reassured his troops that, right or wrong, they were winning the battle.

A thunderous noise accompanied by a sudden jolt rocked the wall below their position knocking down many of the troops, including Charles. Pieces of brick and gray dust showered the rampart. As he lay there, Charles brushed off the brick dust and moved his hand over his body, fearing he had been hit, but found no evidence he was wounded. Then it occurred to him. The French also had cannons. A cannonball had hit the wall below where they were standing. A few meters higher and he might have been killed.

As the terrible pandemonium intensified, his instinct for survival took over. He couldn't fire fast enough and now began to see some of the French troops below firing back as they clambered to retreat. Firing his musket was the only thing he could do to survive and he didn't care if he might be killing men who, like he, had no say in provoking the battle they were now fighting.

He lost all track of time. The firing from below decreased, but Charles kept firing until Ossoli told his men to cease fire. The smoke cleared, giving him his first full view of the residue of a battle. He could not believe what he saw and heard.

Over three hundred bodies were scattered over the ground below, many motionless, others writhing in pain. The pitiful screams and pleas for help of the wounded barely alive shocked him. What affected him most were the cries of men pleading for someone to kill them to end their pain.

Charles slid down to the rampart and sat there muttering over and over to himself, "So this is war. How pathetic. The stupidity of war." His mouth was dry, his ears were ringing, and he could barely hear the voices around him. It felt as though his ears were plugged.

He looked to his left and saw Smyth sitting on the rampart looking straight ahead, staring at the opposite parapet. On his right Piero was checking his musket. Smyth did not move or speak for at least ten minutes before he said, "I can't believe what I've done. I don't think I can ever do that again." Then Ossoli came up to them to congratulate them on their performance and bravery. He appeared energized by the battle and looked anxious to continue fighting. It must be an inherited quality, thought Charles, the result of generations of ancestors who had defended the popes, only this time one of their progeny was opposing the pope.

When he stood he saw a few men had also died on the wall. All he could think was it could have been him. Two men from his platoon were wounded and being cared for by Piero. This made him think of Maria and her work at the hospital. They would be busy today.

General Oudinot, soundly defeated at the Porta Pertusa, divided his remaining troops, one group to move south to the Porta Pancrazio, where Garibaldi had positioned his troops, and the other to proceed north and east along the Vatican wall to the Porta Angelica near the Basilica of St. Peter.

Again, the French General's intelligence reports proved to be incorrect. Over one thousand clerics were still in Rome and the French thought they would unite to open the gate at Porta Angelica and welcome them. Instead his troops suffered heavy losses as they moved along the Vatican wall. The gates of Porta Angelica never opened.

Garibaldi watched from the high ground of the Villa Corsini, outside the walls of the city as the rest of Oudinot's troops approached the Porta Pancrazio. His scouts reported two thousand more French troops protecting Oudinot's flank marched in the same direction. Garibaldi called for his reserve troops from the city. With the reinforcements and using the high ground of the Villa Corsini to his advantage, Garibaldi and his core of redshirts surprised and routed the French who retreated back toward Civitavecchia.

At the end of the day, more than nine hundred French troops died and over three hundred captured. Garibaldi was anxious to pursue them to Civitavecchia, but Mazzini would not permit him to continue.

Charles had to remain on duty at the city wall for another two days to be prepared for a possible return of the French, but they continued on to Civitavecchia. As soon as he was relived from duty he went to the hospital on Tiber Island. More reminders of the horrors of war awaited him there.

There were wounded soldiers filling all the beds and others lying on the floor everywhere. This included many French soldiers. Nuns, the only neutral clerics in Rome, dashed about attending the wounded and dying. Doctors in their blood-spattered frocks looked tired and overworked. A nauseating stench of rotting flesh filled the place. The severely wounded, often delirious, hallucinated and cried out for help or their families, most often their mothers.

He found Maria on the second floor. When she saw him, she ran across the room into his arms and said, "Oh my love, you're alive. I've been so afraid you would be brought in with the wounded and when I didn't see you, I could only think the worst."

"I'm fine, only tired. You look tired too. Have you had any sleep?"

"A little, but we've been too busy to sleep much. Things have settled down. The day of the battle was crazy. Now there are many men with fevers. The doctors tell me it's because their wounds are developing the first stages of gangrene."

"Can you come home with me?"

"Let me ask Margaret. Oh, is Ossoli alright? She hasn't heard from him"

"He's fine. He's a brave man."

"Wonderful, that's good news. I'll tell her and be right back," she said and told him to wait downstairs. It didn't take long before she returned.

"Do you ever get used to that smell?"

"You have no choice other than to open the shutters. It helps. We've been told the French have left. Is it true?"

"Yes, they're gone. We won the battle."

"You're my hero. You fought for Rome and Italy. Thank you."

"Yes, I fought, but am not a hero. The best I can say is I survived."

"No, you're a hero Charles. You didn't have to do this. You could have left like Brown. I would have gone with you. You stayed and I know it was because of me. Not many women have husbands who will risk so much for their wives."

Brushing aside the praise, Charles said, "Looks like you and Margaret did a good job."

"It was difficult at first. When we arrived at the hospital, she was not accepted by the doctors and other men. They didn't like Mazzini's choice of putting a woman in charge, but once the casualties began arriving, all that was forgotten. She did a magnificent job with the resources available on such short notice. The nuns were the real heroes. Not one complaint from any of them. They are the ones who took charge and many men are still alive because of them."

"It's over for now."

"I thought you said we won and the French have left?"

"I did, but I'm convinced they'll be back. For some reason they began by attacking a sealed gate and after they were repelled there, made more bad decisions."

"Do you think they'll be back soon?"

"They probably have more troops back in Civitavecchia. My guess is they'll return with reinforcements," said Charles. "When, I have no idea."

Back at the apartment, he collapsed on the bed and fell into a deep sleep. Maria stayed up a while thinking about what he had said. Was there going to be another battle? Worrying about him and administering to all the casualties affected her more than she let on. The images of the severely wounded still haunted her and although exhausted, she had difficulty sleeping.

CHAPTER TEN

The French Siege

C harles didn't get out of bed until noon the next day. Maria was sleeping so soundly he decided not to disturb her. Reinvigorated after taking a sponge bath, he walked to the neighborhood trattoria for lunch, a place where he had always felt welcome. But today, as soon as he entered the owner started clapping, followed by applause and cheers from the patrons.

Puzzled, Charles asked the owner why the surprising welcome. He answered, "Because you're a hero. Your assistants told us you were a member of the Civic Guard and fought the French. In our way, we're welcoming you as a fellow Roman. Thank you for what you did," answered the owner.

"*Grazie, grazie,*" said Charles bowing slightly to the patrons. As soon as he sat down two men joined him and asked to hear all about the battle. Charles told of his days on the city wall as best he could. He was now accepted as a Roman, but his personality remained American and he did little to embellish the account. When he returned to his studio he received a similar greeting from his carvers and assistants. From that day on all his relations with his Roman companions, friendly enough in the past, but at times taciturn, were warmer.

His absence from the studio left him behind in his work. If the French returned, they would bring a larger army and the Civic Guard would once again be activated to defend the city. There was no way to predict how long a second battle would last and he needed to finish the commissions quickly. If he were to die in battle he wanted to leave Maria with as much money as possible. The carvers didn't have to be told and understood his sense of urgency.

She came to the studio see him later in the day and said, "You should have woken me before you left. I didn't get out of bed until two."

"You were in a deep sleep and I thought you needed the rest. Are you going somewhere?"

"I promised Margaret I'd return to help at the hospital. I'll be back at dinner time. It's already late, but I know she needs help."

The next threat to Rome came from the south. King Ferdinand of Naples was massing his troops on the southern border of the Papal States preparing to march to Rome and return Pio Nono to power. Garibaldi, always aggressive, decided to attack them and disrupt their plan.

Garibaldi had finished routing the French only three days before, and now was rushing into another battle. He left with two thousand men to engage ten thousand Neopolitan troops. Charles thought it was madness.

But Garibaldi had no intention of having his troops engage the Neopolitan army in a conventional battle. Instead, he used guerilla warfare tactics, with surprise attacks by smaller cadres of troops. He often attacked the Neapolitans at night and from different directions. They never knew from where the next ambush would come and called him 'the red devil'. The tactic was successful and Ferdinand's demoralized troops eventually withdrew. Garibaldi asked to pursue the fleeing army all the way to Naples, but again, Mazzini recalled him to Rome.

While Garibaldi fought in the south, France sent an ambassador to Rome to negotiate a possible truce. Embarrassed by their recent defeat they had no intention of making peace with the Republic of Rome, but were making plans to attack the city again, this time with reinforcements of over twenty thousand troops. The negotiations would give them time to move their troops and prepare for a second attempt to enter Rome.

Maria continued to help Margaret at the hospital every day and on returning home one day, Maria asked Charles, "Did you hear anything about the riots today?"

"No. I was busy all day in the studio. What happened?"

"Anticlerical feelings are strong. You've seen *Down with the Jesuits* painted on walls in the city. Today a group vandalized a church. They dragged the confessionals out of a church and were going to burn them in the Piazza del Popolo, but the police stopped them."

"Who told you?"

"I stopped to see Donatangelo on the way home. He also said six priests were shot in Trastevere."

"Rome doesn't need this kind of disorder. It should be preparing for the next attack that I believe is inevitable."

"So, does Margaret. Mazzini told her he also expects the Austrians to attack Rome from the north."

"The French on the west side of the city and the Austrians on the north. What chance do we have? Smyth stopped to see me today. He agrees with me. Rome is in for another battle. He's returning to England tomorrow. I wished him luck and told him I'd miss him, but understood."

"Are you telling me you want to leave?"

"No, I haven't changed my mind," said Charles. "This is our home, and I want us to stay. It may be difficult, but we'll survive."

―――――――

Garibaldi triumphantly marched his troops back into Rome on May 31. On the same day the French ambassador completed an agreement with Mazzini and the other leaders of the Roman Republic allowing the French to encamp outside Rome to protect the city from the Austrians and Neapolitans.

General Oudinot, still smarting from his defeat in April would have nothing to do with the truce and the next day notified the Roman Republic he cancelled the agreement. The French asked for three days for their citizens to leave the city and the Romans agreed.

Two days later, in the middle of the night, the French seized the Villas Corsini and Pamphili overlooking the city, and previously used by Garibaldi to defeat the French in April. The French placed their batteries of cannons on this high ground above Trastevere and prepared to bombard the city.

Deceived by the duplicitous negotiations of the French ambassador, the Romans were unprepared for battle. Having returned only a few days before, Garibaldi's troops were bivouacked throughout the city and he was recuperating from a wound received in the Neapolitan campaign.

Charles and Maria were startled when they were abruptly awoken before dawn Monday, June 1 by the beat of the drums alerting the Civic Guard to report for duty. He couldn't understand why things had changed so fast. The newspapers had reported favorably on the negotiations between the French and Roman Republics. What happened? They had gone to bed assured the French were on their side and would support them if the Austrians attacked Rome.

Maria put her arms around him and embracing him with all her strength said, "You were right, my love. I don't want you to go. I don't want to lose you. This is not your war."

"No, but it's our war. That's naïve bravado, but it's the reality of our situation. You go to the hospital and stay there, as you did in April. I'll look for you there when this is over," said Charles. This did nothing to calm Maria who continued to weep in his arms. Then all the church bells in Rome began ringing in a panicky tempo, adding to their apprehension about what was about to happen to the city.

She accompanied him to the Civic Guard headquarters, where hundreds of couples congregated outside to say their goodbyes. As they held each other both feared the worst. Neither could speak. This unwelcome turn of events seemed to have sapped their emotional energy. After one last kiss, he turned and left to search for his platoon. Maria did not move, watching him until he disappeared into the mass of soldiers.

Charles found Piero who asked, "Do you know anything about Ossoli? And where's Smyth?"

"I've heard nothing, but I'm certain Ossoli is on his way" said Charles. "Smyth is on his way back to England."

"I don't blame him. I'm surprised you're still here."

"To a degree, so am I, but it's too late to change my mind now."

Then they both smiled in relief when they saw Ossoli running toward them.

"Sorry I'm late, but I was getting our orders," he said. "There's no time for a formal assembly. We must leave immediately."

"What happened?" said Piero. "I thought an agreement had been reached with the French. A kind of truce?"

"They were stalling while they brought in reinforcements and have already seized the Villas Corsini, Pamphili, and the adjacent Villa Vallentini," said Ossoli. "Our orders are to return to the wall, this time at the Porta Pancrazio in the area facing Villa Corsini."

The streets were filled with troops, some rushing toward the Porta Pancrazio and others toward the Basilica of St. Peter where Garibaldi's regiment was ordered to assemble in the square. Almost dark when they arrived, they took their positions on the rampart, prepared their muskets, and fixed their bayonets.

Charles could see batteries of cannons positioned on the wall on either side of the gate. Occasional lights flickered on the road leading from the Porta Pancrazio to the Villa Corsini. Otherwise, darkness hid the enemy.

Then, behind him he heard the sound of horses and marching troops. Everyone on the rampart rushed to the opposite side to see Garibaldi leading what looked like thousands of troops up Mount Janiculum toward the Porta Pancrazio. Charles had never seen Garibaldi before, but there he was, riding a white horse and wearing his distinctive red shirt. Next to him, on a chestnut horse was the man people said never left his side, a black man, the legendary giant, Aguyar. He had never seen a man so big. The whole scene sent shivers through his body. The stage was now set for the battle.

The first light of dawn began to illuminate this ominous setting and the men on the rampart were ordered to take to their positions. Charles looked over the parapet and there was now enough light see the French soldiers, about two hundred meters away on the upper floors of the Villa Corsisni. This large four-story villa overlooked a garden with vineyards and cornfields to its right and the Villa Valentini on the opposite side of the road, to its left.

Behind Corsini was a forest of pines and another building on the right seized by the French, the Convent of St. Pancrazio. The road from the gate of the Porta Pancrazio led uphill to the lower garden of Corsini where the main road veered to the right and a path along a low wall continued to the left toward a farmhouse, Casa Giacometti.

Retaking Corsini looked impossible to Charles. There was no cover. The troops would have to charge uphill into a wall of bullets and cannon fire coming from Villa Corsinii above, and crossfire from Villa Valentini to their right.

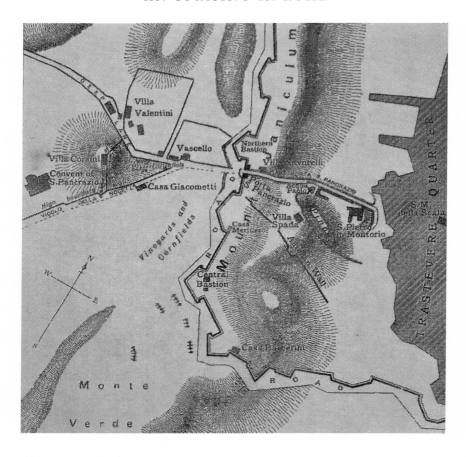

But it didn't matter what he thought. The inevitable was about to begin. As he learned in April, all the troops on the front lines could do was fight for their survival. Kill or be killed. Once the battle began all orders assumed front-line troops were expendable. What did matter to him now was whether he was to become one of the expendables charging up that hill. His speculation ended abruptly when Ossoli shouted, "Prepare to fire. Direct your fire at the Villa Corsini."

Everyone along the line of the parapet braced themselves and readied their muskets. Tense and afraid, the men jumped when the first cannon shot fired. Then a second. After a brief pause came the order from Ossoli to fire. Both the north and south batteries kept up a steady rhythm of deafening cannon shots for at least ten minutes. Then Ossoli shouted, "Cease fire."

A great nightmarish roar rose from Garibaldi's troops staged behind the wall. Charles could hear the massive gate open. Garibaldi and Aguyar were the first out of the gate, pistols in one hand, swords in the other, followed by their troops streaming through the gate, now prodded to a crazed state shouting and waving their weapons. Garibaldi and his core of redshirts from South America moved to either side of this mass of frenzied troops, prepared to keep the line of attack moving forward.

Musket and cannon fire erupted from Villa Corsini. He saw the first wave of Garibaldi's troops cut down by the enemy fire like the clean, swift cut of a scythe mowing wheat. The officers pressed more men forward. Moving farther up the hill they were then caught in the crossfire from the Villa Vallentini, but somehow a few advanced toward Villa Corsini.

Ossoli's men could not join the battle fearing they would hit the troops struggling up the hill. Charles watched in horror as this macabre battlefield dance was replayed by wave after wave of troops able to only gain ground meter by meter. The wall beneath him shook nonstop as the French artillery did their best to breach it. The Italian cannons responded with accurate fire dismantling Villa Corsini piece by piece.

After about an hour Garibaldi's troops were closer to Villa Corsini but pinned down by fire. Suddenly, Garibaldi and Aguyar raced to the front of the troops heading straight toward the Villa Corsini. The troops followed in their wake as Garibaldi led the way up the front steps of the villa. Charles watched in horror at what happened next.

As French soldiers rushed out the door they were cut down by the swords of Garibaldi and Arguyar. A bayonet fight erupted when Garibaldi's troops joined their general. Soldiers from both sides began to fall, but the Italians gained an advantage and Charles could see French troops fleeing out the back of the villa and running into the pine forest. Garibaldi and his troops had won and taken possession of Corsini. The men on the rampart cheered.

But Garibaldi's victory was short-lived. Oudinot had thousands of troops bivouacked in the pine forest and fresh reinforcements charged Villa Corsini overwhelming the Italians. Garibaldi and Aguyar were able to escape the onslaught and fled for cover to the Villa Vascello at the bottom of the hill.

After the Italian retreat, Charles watched in disbelief as Garibaldi ordered more troops to charge Villa Corsini. These futile assaults continued intermittently throughout the rest of the day, but by evening the French, because of their superior strategic position and larger army, repelled all counterattacks by the Italians. Estimates of the Italian casualties from these senseless charges directly into French fire varied from five hundred to nine hundred killed in one day of battle.

Before the last light of day faded, Charles could see the dead bodies of the Italian soldiers covering the hill leading to Villa Corsini. He remembered the sight of all the dead and wounded French troops after the battle in April, and how gruesome that had appeared. This far exceeded anything he could imagine.

Charles worried the memory of these scenes of horror would forever compromise his ability to create or even appreciate beauty. After all, he was an artist, someone who was supposed to understand and represent beauty, not this sickening waste of human life.

When Ossoli came down the line of troops along the wall to see if there were any dead or wounded the reality of Charles's situation overcame him and he knew his only concern must be survival. Ossoli gathered his men and told them, "We have been ordered to leave the wall and support troops guarding the Villa Savarelli on this side of the wall. You have five minutes to get all your gear together before we leave."

Someone asked, "Why there?"

"I don't know, but I'm sure we'll find out," answered Ossoli.

Villa Savarelli was a short distance from the Porta Pancrazio on the north side of Via Pancrazio, the main road leading to the gate, but moving in the dark made the going slow. When they arrived at the villa, Ossoli went inside the villa to report and receive his orders.

A large number of troops surrounded the building making Charles think someone important was inside. On returning, Ossoli confirmed his suspicion. "This is General Garibaldi's headquarters," said Ossoli. "We are to join the troops on the east side of the building. Stay together tonight and in the morning, we'll have a better idea of the layout of the grounds."

After stumbling in the dark over men already asleep Charles, Piero, and Ossoli found a spot to stretch out on the ground about twenty meters from the back of the villa.

"At least when I was in prison I had some straw to sleep on," said Piero. "This ground is hard and bumpy."

"After today," said Charles, "I think I could sleep on a rock. I'm exhausted. Ossoli, do you think we have any chance against the French with all their reinforcements?"

"Let's see what tomorrow brings," said Ossoli avoiding Charles's eyes.

A gentle kick from a soldier distributing bread and cheese woke Charles at dawn. He responded instinctively accepting the food, but it took him several minutes to clear his head. Stretching and rubbing his eyes, the wall he had defended the day before came into focus. What he saw unnerved him.

All his limited experience as a soldier had been spent on the wall, a mighty fortification that made him feel invulnerable. Now, no longer crouched behind a parapet looking down at the enemy, he was looking up at the higher ground held by the French. He could see their cannons in the distance above the other side of the wall. They were pointed at the villa.

Piero nudged him and said, "I liked it better on the wall. This villa is large but it sits on high ground. The architect designed it to dominate the surrounding landscape. He succeeded, but never considered it would make such an easy target for French cannons."

"If those cannons begin firing at the villa, the only cover will be behind it," said Charles. "We won't have a chance if they break through the gate of Porta Pancrazio. Where's Ossoli?"

"He must be inside meeting with the officers," said Piero. "He was already gone when I woke up."

They began to eat their breakfast, but were interrupted when the French cannons commenced firing, the first shot hitting a side of the villa. They rushed for cover behind the building. The firing continued becoming more accurate with shots hitting the front of the villa. Other shots missed but landed in the gardens and stables panicking the horses, who broke free and raced away from the direction of the fire. A section of the stable roof collapsed and the agonizing screams of the trapped stable hands and remaining horses resonated throughout the grounds.

The cannon fire lasted about twenty minutes and left gaping holes scattered over the front of the villa. The French then turned their guns on Trastevere. He and Piero had a clear view of the havoc created by the shelling. Walls and roofs crumbled under the impact of the cannon balls and they could see people running down the streets away from the direction of the shelling. The bombardment continued for the next half hour.

"If their intention is to terrorize the people, they have succeeded," said Charles.

"Killing civilians is inhumane," said Piero, "but I learned long ago leaders shed their humanity when they assume power, like a snake sheds its skin. You can count on it."

"Here comes Ossoli," said Charles.

He came racing around the side of the villa and slumped down beside Charles and Piero.

176

"Are we going to stay here, in the line of fire?" asked Piero.

"Yes, that's our orders," replied Ossoli. "For now, it may be safer than being on the wall. The French are reportedly moving troops farther south. Garibaldi thinks they are not planning to attempt to breach the wall at Porta Pancrazio, but near the Central Bastion further south."

"Then what?" asked Charles.

"If they breach the wall then the battle moves onto the Janiculum," said Ossolli. "If we cannot stop them here, Rome will be theirs."

The shelling of the villa and Rome continued. Dirty, hungry, and tired Charles began to wonder how much more of this battle he could endure. Ossoli did his best to protect his men, but he could see the doubt in their eyes.

He and Piero would pass the time between the periods of bombardment and sentry duty talking about sculpture. They would challenge each other to describe a new monument and how they would plan its construction including the type of marble used and the number of carvers and helpers required to complete it. This helped pass the time during the day, but in the quiet of the night he could only think of Maria and whether he would ever hold his love again.

The Roman troops were able to hold their ground until the 20th of June, when everything changed. The French began a major offensive to breach the wall. As anticipated, they chose the area of the central bastion, south of Porta Pancrazio. Charles could see men on the wall covering the rampart with brush to be set fire if the French reached the top. Despite of all their efforts, the French cannons succeeded in collapsing a section of the wall and driving the Italians from the rampart.

The next morning Charles could see the breached area of the wall. During the night the French covered the piles of fallen bricks with mounds of dirt and French troops were now swarming over the earthen bridge. The Italians retreated to the remains of the old Aurelian wall where Garibaldi decided they would make their stand.

Watching all this, Charles knew their turn to join the battle against this massive influx of French troops would come. It did not take long before it happened. Ossoli came from the villa, now in ruins, and said, "We're leaving here and moving to the Villa Spada closer to the Aurelian wall where Garibaldi is moving his headquarters."

Their platoon joined about two hundred other troops moving to the Villa Spada. It was a three-story villa, smaller than Servalli, but set in a large garden encircled by a low wall. Once in position they were joined by Garibaldi and his redshirts. There was no fighting that day, but during the night Charles could hear sporadic gunfire of French patrols harassing the Italian troops along the Aurelian wall.

The final battle to defend the Roman Republic began the next morning. The Italian troops on the Aurelian wall fought bravely, but were outnumbered at least five to one. Relentless French cannon fire pummeled Villa Spada. Garibaldi would leave the battered villa at least once a day and ride up and down the line of defenders on the wall to bolster their morale.

After nine days the Italians could no longer contain the onslaught of French troops. They had overrun the Aurelian wall at several points and would soon be moving toward Villa Spada. Charles saw Garibaldi leave, but without his longtime friend and protector, Aguyar, who must have been killed. As he watched the great general and his staff depart, he was certain this is where he would die. Ossoli was left in charge of the remaining troops for their final defense of what was left of the battered villa.

Some troops had fled, others had been killed, leaving only ninety-five. Ossoli had them take positions on the second and third floor at the numerous gaping holes in the walls left from the shelling. Charles, Piero, and forty others were assigned to the third floor.

The floor was covered with chunks of wall, ceiling, or other debris. He and Piero stacked this debris where a window destroyed by cannon fire left an opening facing the Aurelian wall. They positioned themselves behind their shield of debris and prepared for the final defense of Villa Spada.

"You shouldn't be here," said Piero. "I regret agreeing with Donatangelo when he suggested you join Maria and I for our adventure in Civitavecchia. From then on even though you weren't one of us, your collaboration with our cause led you to this grand finale of our revolution, not yours. Ossoli and I should be here, not you."

"But I'm here. This isn't a time to look back on how I ended up here. I'm not about to give up and I know you aren't either," said Charles trying unsuccessfully to control the fear in his voice.

They had a clear view of the final stages of the battle before them. By mid-afternoon they watched as the Italians lost total control of the wall and were surrendering en masse. It was not until after four o'clock they could see about three hundred French troops assembling for what looked like an assault on Villa Spada.

Charles had never been, nor did he think he would ever be, as afraid as at that moment. About three hundred troops, all determined to kill them, were preparing to attack the villa. Even the sky filled with dark clouds was intimidating. When he looked over at Piero the hopelessness of the situation was obvious on his face and in his eyes. Ossoli moved up and down what remained of the stairs encouraging his men and telling them to use their limited ammunition wisely and hold their fire until he gave the order.

About one hundred yards from the villa the French split into four groups preparing to attack from all sides. Their best cover would be the low wall encircling the garden and that's where they headed. No order from Ossoli came to fire. An eerie silence and further darkening of the sky, changes that often portend a powerful summer thunderstorm, enveloped the garden. Then one of the French soldiers jumped the garden wall and ran toward the back of the villa. Other French soldiers began firing to cover his solo attack. Ossoli ordered the men in the rear of the building to fire and the French intruder dropped.

The French opened fire from all sides of the garden. Ossoli ran from floor to floor shouting, "Fire, Fire!" Momentarily terrified, Charles reacted from panic, firing without thinking or aiming, but when he saw French troops running toward the villa he recognized either he stopped them or they would soon be running up the stairs. It was no longer time to think, it was time to resurrect the instinct to kill or be killed.

They were outnumbered, but had the advantage of fighting from higher ground and the cover of their mutilated villa fortress. They were winning, but the French, in spite of heavy losses, refused to retreat. He knew they would eventually overrun Villa Spada. Any French soldier who reached the lower level of the villa and attempted to charge up the stairs was greeted by a pistol shot from Ossoli. If one of his men were hit, Ossoli grabbed their musket and ammunition and gave it to one of the others. He seemed to be everywhere, supporting and inspiring his men.

What came next caught both sides by surprise. A sudden flash of lightening, followed by a sharp ear-splitting crack of thunder, caused everyone to stop firing and look up. First, scattered large drops of rain fell, then further blackening of the sky, followed by a heavy downpour drenching the French troops and interrupting their fire. Despite the damage to the roof of the villa the troops inside were spared from the worst of the downpour and continued to fire at the French as they retreated from the garden toward the Aurelian wall.

It had all changed in a moment and Charles considered it a miracle. The lightening, thunder, and downpour intensified as the darkness deepened. All the men on the third floor jumped up and cheered the rain. Charles had never seen such a beautiful storm.

Ossoli came running up the stairs ordering everyone to assemble on the ground floor. When they were all together he said, "I'm proud of what you did today. We stopped the French, but we could see our troops along the wall were defeated and many captured. We're outnumbered and have no reserve to support us. Everyone is free to leave under the cover of this storm. If anyone wishes to stay I'll not stop them, but it's time to accept the reality of the French victory. Head back to the city where we may have a chance to regroup. You have an advantage, you know this terrain better than the French. We'll be more likely to reach the city if we move in small groups. Good luck."

As far as Charles was concerned it was the greatest speech he had ever heard. The men scattered at once and Ossoli waited until everyone had left. Charles and Piero waited with him before the three set out into the storm running, stumbling, and slipping in the mud across the open field toward Via Pancrazio. They were not alone. Hundreds of Italian troops were taking advantage of the propitious storm and fleeing toward Rome.

The downpour continued as they reached Via Pancrazio and turned toward Trastevere. Piero said, "I'll leave you here. I'm going to find Donatangelo. Ossoli, what do you think our chances of stopping the French are?"

"I know Garibaldi has been meeting with Mazzini and the other leaders," said Ossoli. "The last time he returned from Rome, I overheard him say they had come to a final decision. You saw for yourself the mass flight of Italian troops. I know Garibaldi realized he didn't have enough troops to defend Rome if the French entered the city. I'll let you reach your own conclusion."

Looking dejected, Piero said, "Surrender is the only conclusion."

"I agree," said Ossoli.

"Meaning we could become prisoners of the French?" said Charles.

"There's no way I'm going back to prison," said Piero. "That's why I want to find Donatangelo and return to my underground life. Charles you're an American. You can claim you never were a part of this battle."

"Yes," said Ossoli. You can return to your studio and go on with your work. Destroy your uniform when you get there. They won't bother you as long as you have your papers."

"What about you?" Charles asked Ossoli.

"I'm not sure. My family background makes it difficult to hide my participation in the Civic Guard," said Ossoli.

"But Margaret is an American. You're married, aren't you?"

"We are married. We were married in Rieti, but never told anyone. For now, I have no answer. We'd better keep moving."

Piero left and Charles and Ossoli went on to the hospital where they hoped to find their wives. The bridge across the Tiber was packed with Roman troops considering the same grim possibilities discussed by the three.

They found the hospital filled with more casualties than in April. Maria spotted the two and came running to embrace Charles. She would not let go for the longest time until Charles said, "Let's go. You look exhausted."

"I am, but seeing you has made me so happy, I've already forgot how tired I was. Let me find Margaret and tell her I'm leaving."

When she walked away he looked around and almost broke into tears at what he saw. Every space on the blood-spattered floor was occupied by wounded. The few beds in the room held the more seriously injured. Blood-soaked bandages covered limbs, torsos, and heads. Their faces expressed dismay, and helplessness, an image etched in his mind from that day on.

There were dead bodies they did not yet have time to remove. Once again before him was the tragic residue of war, the only ones who paid the price for whatever diplomatic disagreement or cause that led to a confrontation. Most likely few in the room, alive or dead, again, had any idea why they were fighting.

Then he felt a tug on his arm and Maria said, "What were you thinking about. I had to shake you three times to get your attention."

"I have to get out of here," said Charles.

"So do I," she said. "I haven't left since you went to fight the beginning of the month."

When they crossed into the city he said, "I feel I should kiss the pavement. I doubted I would ever return to these streets."

"Let's not talk about that now, I only want to get back to our apartment and our life," said Maria. Few neighborhoods had been spared from the persistent French bombardment and many streets were impassable. People were scavenging through the rubble for their buried possessions, or worse, were looters. Both feared what they would find when they reached their apartment.

Nearing home, they quickened their pace. When their building came into view they ran and were relieved to see it was undamaged. Maria rushed into the apartment and he ran to check his two studios. The studio below the apartment was undamaged, but the second studio, down the street was.

He had to struggle to force the door open, and when he did, all he could see was a pile of wooden beams and shattered stone. The two commissions, if they were still intact, would be somewhere under the rubble. Charles sat down on a large shattered piece of the wall and wept. All he had been through the past month, the fighting, the killing, the terror, and now the destruction of his work, overwhelmed him.

He remembered how Piero wept when he was released from his year of hell. He had thought he understood Piero's anguish at the time. But now realized he didn't. Before, evil was something that happened to others or something he read about in books or newspapers. It had never had a face or being. All this had changed him. Why hadn't he left for America with Maria? Retrospect, he concluded, was easy, but reality difficult and unpredictable. He began to sob.

Maria's came rushing through the door shouting, "Oh *dio mio*, what have they done?" She could tell he had been crying, put her arms around him and hugged him, saying, "We can fix this, we can fix this. You're safe. That's all that matters. Let's go back to the apartment."

He said nothing on the walk, back but when Maria shut the door he said, "Ossoli told me the first thing I should do is burn my uniform"

"Why?" she asked.

"Rome is lost. When the French occupy the city, they'll be looking for anyone who served in the army or Civic Guard and put them in prison."

"You're an American, they can't do that."

"I'm taking no chances," said Charles who began undressing.

"You're filthy," said Maria. "Let me start boiling some water for your bath."

"Here, you can use my uniform to light the fire.

"What about Ossoli and Piero?"

"Because he's an officer in the Civic Guard, Ossoli is concerned. And Piero, he's safe, but left to find Donatangelo. We may not see him for a while," said Charles.

When both finished their baths and were about to go to bed they were surprised by a knock on the door. They looked at one another nervously and hesitated to answer. Charles asked Maria if she had burned the uniform and she nodded. The knocking persisted but didn't have the demanding sound one would expect if it were a soldier or policeman.

Charles opened the door cautiously and was surprised to see Piero. "What happened? I thought you were going to find Donatangelo."

"I did go to the cameo workshop. It was destroyed in the shelling of Trastevere," said Piero. "The walls collapsed as did the building next door. I found someone in the neighborhood who told me there were no survivors. Donatangelo is probably buried in the cellar under all the rubble. My studio was also hit. Can you help me? It seems we did this before."

"Of course, come in," said Charles.

When she heard Piero's voice Maria came running to the door and hugging him said, "I overheard what you said about Dontangelo. How awful."

"I guess my plans have changed. Perhaps I can stay in one of your studios tonight."

"You're welcome to stay in the apartment," said Maria, "for as long as you like."

"I'm leaving tomorrow, so I'll only be here tonight."

Surprised, Charles asked, "Where are you going? I think you should rest after what we've been through. Besides, the French will be occupying the city in a day or two and you should stay off the streets. You don't want to be thrown in prison again."

"The French won't have a chance to capture me. Garibaldi has let it be known he's not abandoning the struggle for Italian unification and is looking for volunteers to join his troops and lead them north to join the fight against the Austrians. I've decided to follow him."

Piero's decision caught Charles by surprise and the image of all the dead Italian troops on the hill leading to Villa Corsini came back as he pleaded with his friend, "The French must have an army of twenty thousand troops in the area and the Austrians are on the northern border of the Papal States. Garibaldi is marching into a trap. Please stay with us until the situation calms down."

"I have no intention of being captured here. I've been through too much to give up our dream. People want change."

"Stay and continue your work here in Rome," Charles begged. "You're an important member of Young Italy. When things settle down you can continue your work with them. That's what Donatangelo would want. And what about your gift as an artist and sculptor?"

"I must continue what we began. These battles we've fought against the French are the beginning of the final campaign for unification of the peninsula. I'm convinced of that," said Piero with a fierce look of pride. "Once, I wanted to be a sculptor. My year in prison, and everything I've experienced since, has destroyed that dream.

"It's like waking up in the morning and trying to remember the dream you had last night. You know you had one, but can't remember where or what it was all about. No more marble to carve and admire. I'll only be able to sit back and admire what I've done when we've succeeded in overthrowing the despots and unifying our country."

Charles now knew it would be useless to believe he could save his friend from the possible tragedy that might await Garibaldi and his troops. He agreed the people wanted change, but he thought the 'beginning' Piero believed in was an overture to a long bloody war about to encompass all of Italy. He looked at Maria, who without saying a word, made it clear to him the discussion was over.

The following morning, they decided to accompany Piero to St. Peter's Square where Garibaldi's volunteers were assembling. The streets were chaotic. The people of Rome had no idea what to expect when the French entered the city and were preparing for the worst. Others were also on their way to volunteer for Garibaldi's army accompanied by mothers, wives, or lovers. Mothers of young boys cried and pleaded on their knees to their sons not to follow Garibaldi.

When they reached St. Peter's, similar scenes were occurring throughout the square. After they finally said their tearful goodbyes, Piero left to see if he could find any of his friends from the Civic Guards.

Cheering erupted at the entrance of the street leading into the square and everyone turned and rushed toward the shouts. Coming down the street wearing a red tunic and the characteristic black feathers in his hat was Garibaldi. People surrounded his white horse as he slowly inched his way to the obelisk in the center of the square. He raised his gloved hand silencing the crowd, and said:

"Fortune who betrays us today, will smile on us tomorrow. I am going out of Rome. Let those who wish to continue the war against the stranger, come with me. I offer neither pay, nor quarters, nor provisions; I offer hunger, thirst, forced marches, battles and death. Let him who loves his country in his heart and not with his lips only, follow me."

Joined by his staff of redshirts, his wife Anitra and their infant child, and the populist Ciceruacchio, Garibaldi led his army of volunteers out of the square and through the streets of Rome. They were greeted with cheers of adulation making it sound as though they had won the battle for Rome, not the French.

Watching the volunteers marching out of the square reminded Charles he was losing his best friend. He and Piero had studied together with Professor Morretti, drank together at the Caffé Greco, and fought the French side-by-side. He had introduced him to the exciting underground world of an Italian secret society, but best of all, he had introduced him to Maria. Piero changed a once innocent American's life in many ways, and Charles would be forever grateful for having the good fortune to have had him as a friend.

───────────

When the French marched into the city two days later, they still thought they would be welcomed by Pio Nono's admirers, but their only supporters were all clergy. The Romans could never forgive the French for their bombardment of the city. They were unwelcome occupiers.

In an attempt to intimidate the Romans, the French marched their troops up and down the streets of Rome for the next two days and imposed a curfew of 9:30. Anyone suspected of being an Italian soldier was seized and sent to prison. They dismissed the top government officials but did not jail them. Even Mazzini was free to go where he pleased, but after two weeks left for the north.

Charles would not allow Maria to leave the apartment for the first week of the occupation. She was worried about Margaret and Ossoli and on the eighth day of the occupation, convinced him to take her to their apartment. On their way, they were stopped twice by soldiers who paid more attention to Maria than Charles. When he answered them in English, they would smile and walk away.

As soon as they entered the Ossoli's apartment they saw travel trunks in the hall.

"Where are you going?" asked a surprised Maria as she hugged Margaret.

"We're leaving for Rieti tomorrow to pick up Nino and then going on to Florence," said Margaret.

"Please, come in and sit down," said Ossoli, joining them from another room. "We were thinking about coming to visit you, but there are too many troops on the streets. I haven't been out of the house since the French occupied the city."

"A good idea. We were stopped twice on the way here. When I spoke to them and they realized I was American, they walked away and left us alone. Do you think you'll have any trouble leaving the city?"

"We hope not," said Margaret. "After the fighting began in in April, Washington sent a special envoy to report on the situation and to help any Americans in Rome who needed to leave the city. The special envoy and James Winton prepared the necessary papers. Winton has been most helpful. You should contact him before you make any plans to leave."

"We hate to see you leave, but I think it's the right decision," said Charles.

"I agree," said Maria. "Today is the first day I've been out and there are French soldiers everywhere looking for any excuse to cause trouble. Margaret, I'm going to miss you."

"And I'll miss you. What are your plans?"

"I have commissions to finish, and then I'm going to take Maria to America to meet my family," said Charles. "One of my studios was badly damaged in the bombardment, so that will delay our departure, but we're definitely going."

"When do you plan to leave for America?" asked Maria.

"Probably not until spring," said Margaret. "Perhaps you'll also be ready to leave by that time. We could cross the Atlantic together. Why don't you come to Florence when Charles has finished his commissions?"

"That's a possibility," said Charles. Maria nodded her head in agreement.

It was difficult for the two couples to say goodbye. What they had been through together the past six months left them with a permanent bond of friendship they did not wish to see end.

CHAPTER ELEVEN

America via Florence

Charles returned to work and began removing the rubble from the damaged studio. They were able to salvage the two commissions, both in their early stages of development, but it took over a month and then another month to move them to the other studio.

He devoted all his time to completing the commissions. If there were no complications, he felt he could finish in five to six months. He doubted there would be any new commissions since there wouldn't be many American tourists visiting Rome during all this unrest.

The next time Charles met James Winton at the Caffé Greco he noticed a difference in the usually jovial atmosphere and asked, "Where's everybody? The place looks empty."

"So many artists were killed after they volunteered to fight with Gaibaldi," said Winton.

"I was there. I didn't realize there were so many artists with Garibaldi. I watched the massacre. It could have been stopped. There was no way Garibaldi could take and hold Villa Corsini."

"Artists tend to be impulsive idealists. They had no idea what they were facing," said Winton. "I'm so glad to see you. When Smyth told me you were going to continue serving with the Civic Guard I was concerned. Oudinot and the French were not about to be embarrassed a second time."

"Enough about those tragic days. I'm trying to forget them. Tell me what you're hearing from the other embassies concerning the return of Pio Nono."

"He will return to Rome. The big question is when? The Cardinals are returning to power, and as before, will be running the government and the Chamber of Deputies, which at the moment is powerless to do anything. The Roman Republic no longer exists. To sum it up, the French have restored the temporal power of the Pope and what began last November until now was a brief pause in the centuries-old rule of the Papacy."

Charles stared down in his drink for a long time before saying, "I'm sorry, but it's difficult for me to accept the situation after all I witnessed in the battle. So much death and destruction and no change. How can anyone justify all that carnage to the families of the dead and wounded?"

"You can't. You must go on with your life."

"I have a favor to ask of you."

"How can I help you?"

"I plan to take Maria to America in the spring. I want to be sure we have all the right papers for her and that mine are up to date."

"That should be no problem, particularly because you have given me plenty of notice."

"Thanks for all your help. I want you to come to the studio."

"Is there something special to see?" asked Winton.

"No, but I'd like to make a marble bust of you. I need you to sit for the initial clay maquette."

"A bust of me?"

"Yes, you've been kind to me and Maria. You made my career and for that I'll be forever grateful."

"Thank you. It was obvious to me you were talented. If I have any tourists stop at the office, I'll be sure to send them to your studio, but currently, tourists from America are scarce."

The Roman Republic was a fast fading memory and even though Pio Nono had not yet returned, life in the city went on as though he had never left. The cardinals and clerics once more dominated the political scene and the major change on the streets was the presence of French troops. After a month, satisfied they were in control, the French ended the curfew.

Charles completed and shipped his commissions in early December, but with no new work, he quickly became restless. Their friends were gone and with nothing to keep him occupied Maria became concerned. From the day they had met, their life had been a nonstop adventure. They needed to make plans for a new life. Participating in the activity of Young Italy was no longer an option for Maria. It was too dangerous with the French in control.

A letter from Margaret, now in Florence, offered a possible solution to their current inertia. She wanted them to travel to America with them, admitting she needed someone like Maria to help her with Nino during the crossing. Margaret added she had met a prominent sculptor in Florence, Hiram Powers, who had an excellent reputation. He told her Charles would be welcome to come and work with him until they left for America.

After reading the letter Charles said, "Powers has always been popular with American tourists. Every American stopping in Florence seems to have visited his studio. They all talked about him when they came to visit mine. We have to wait until spring before we leave anyway. I like the idea. Let's make the crossing with Ossoli and Margaret."

They were ready to depart for Florence after Christmas. Maria's papers were in order, but both had second thoughts when it came time to leave their comfortable apartment and the memories of their years together in Rome. Maria wondered if she would ever see to Rome again. On the cold winter morning they left, not a word was said as they passed through the streets. When their carriage exited Porta

Angelica into the Campagna Maria gave one quick look back and then buried her head on Charles's shoulder.

⸻

Charles had been to Florence and the marble quarries outside of Pietrasanta and Carrara during the year he studied with Professor Morretti. For Maria this was a new world. Margaret found them a small, but comfortable apartment in her neighborhood across the Arno River from the center of Florence. Charles liked the location and the price.

The first thing they did was visit the Ossolis. "I'm so pleased you agreed to come to Florence and join us for our crossing," said Margaret. "Nino is more than I can handle. Giovanni does help me, but you know how Italian men can be. They adore their children, but do it on their schedule. It's difficult to find time to write."

"I'll make you a bargain. You show me this city and in return I'll take care of Nino in the morning during the week."

In an instant Margaret said, "Agreed," and they both laughed.

"I'm grateful to you for arranging for Charles to meet Hiram Powers. He becomes unhappy if he's idle for any length of time. He needs to work."

"I'll take him to meet Powers tomorrow."

Charles and Ossoli spent the rest of the afternoon discussing the changes in Rome under the French occupation. It was the first opportunity for Maria to see Nino. After his afternoon nap, she took him in her arms and they immediately bonded. She longed for her own child, but until that happened and she prayed every day it would, caring for Nino would be her joy. At the end of the day it was the kind of welcome she needed after the anxiety she felt leaving her home in Rome.

Charles was awed when he saw Powers's studio located in a building the size of a small palazzo. The décor on the inside was as impressive. A servant took them through a small inner courtyard to a back building where they found Powers, a big man with a large beard, at work in his studio.

"This is the American sculptor from Rome I mentioned to you," said Margaret.

"Welcome to Florence.," said Powers. "Margaret said you studied with Morretti."

"I did and have been working out of my own studio the past three years," said Charles. "I've heard a great deal about you from the Americans who pass through Rome."

"I hope it was good," said Powers with a hearty laugh. "As you can see, I have more than enough work to keep me busy and you're welcome to work in the studio. Perhaps we can learn something from each other."

There were at least ten assistants working in the busy studio. Charles was impressed with the quality of work, fifty percent of which were busts. He gladly accepted Powers's offer.

Maria and Charles had no problem adjusting to their new life in Florence. The city offered another world of art and sculpture for Charles to study and Nino loved his new part time nanny. Powers proved not only be a good sculptor, but also someone who enjoyed inventing new tools for his craft. He and Charles would spend hours debating the pros and cons of different chisels or the choice of what type of abrasive to use for the final finishing of the surface of various marbles. As Powers had suggested they both learned something new.

Another benefit to working in Powers's studio was the steady flow of American tourists through Florence. When one of the visitors, a senator from Maryland, heard Charles was a sculptor and on his way home to Washington he said to him, "We don't have trained American sculptors at home. All the American marble sculptors are either studying or working in Italy. We have to recruit carvers from Italy to do the work, and there is going to be even more work soon.

The members of Congress are complaining about all the jobs going to the Italian carvers."

"You said there was going to be even more work. What exactly do you mean?" asked Charles.

"Congress recently passed a bill approving a major expansion of the Capitol building that will take years to complete. I want you to come to see me when you return to Washington," said the senator. "You have the training, and we want American sculptors to work on this expansion. This would be a great opportunity for you to be part of the team. Promise you'll stop to see me."

"Thanks for the offer. When I get back to Washington, I promise I'll visit your office," said Charles.

Powers joined them and said to the senator, "I understand Senator John C. Calhoun of South Carolina died three weeks ago?"

"He did. What a great loss. He was one of our finest senators and interpreters of our constitution. He rarely lost a debate and also served as Vice President twice. A great man," said the senator.

"Let me show you a sculpture I've done of the distinguished Senator Calhoun. It was commissioned by the city of Charleston several years ago and is ready to ship."

Powers led them to a room off the main studio where he uncovered a life-sized marble sculpture of Calhoun. The senator from Maryland gasped before he said, "That's him all right. It's wonderful. The likeness is astonishing. I was unaware he came to Italy to pose for this."

"He didn't. They sent me a plaster bust made from a life mask done in Charleston. Greatness is written all over his face. I decided to drape the figure in a toga, symbolizing his political genius and eminence as a leader of our emerging democracy," said Powers. "He chose the words on the scroll held in his left hand—Truth, Justice, and the Constitution."

"They'll love it in South Carolina. What a great tribute and what an appropriate time for it to arrive in Charleston," said the senator. "When will it be shipped?"

"It will leave Livorno May 17th with a stop in New York first."

When the senator left Charles asked Powers the details about the ship taking the sculpture to America.

The next day as he and Ossoli were enjoying an afternoon aperitif, Charles told him he found a ship leaving from Livorno on May 17. It sounded perfect for the four of them. It was a three-masted cargo schooner sailing for New York and had room for six passengers. A friend told him the accommodations and service were better than on the steamships because there were so few passengers on cargo ships. The cost was also less than a steamship, but the trip would take longer.

The two couples met on a Sunday afternoon to discuss Charles's proposal. Margaret and Maria liked the idea of the small number of passengers. They all liked the price compared to the usual steamship rates and decided to do it.

Later, sitting outside by the Arno enjoying the April sunshine with Nino, it occurred to Maria she would be leaving for America in six weeks. She had never been on a large boat, never on the Mediterranean Sea, or more frightening, the Atlantic Ocean. She had heard many stories about how awful sea sickness could be. And would Charles's family accept her? All this caused her a sudden sense of panic. After a few minutes she calmed down, but these uncertainties would persist until she reached America.

The big news in Florence in April was Pio Nono's return to Rome. Charles could not understand why it took him almost fourteen months to return. The French were there to protect him. No one believed it would be the same liberal Pio Nono who had made so many concessions to the people of the Papal States before he fled.

Ossoli told Charles he would never go back to Rome until the pope relinquished his temporal power over the Papal States. "In other words, I'll never be returning to Rome. Not only Pio Nono, but my entire family do not want me to return. I'm an embarrassment to them for supporting the revolution of Mazzini and Garibaldi."

The mention of Garibaldi made Charles think of Piero. Was he still alive? He might never know. Garibaldi's attempt to continue the revolution failed and he disbanded his army within a month after leaving Rome. He then fled to America.

May 1, 1850 the two couples began packing for their voyage to America. The excitement or anxiety in Maria's case, increased until they boarded the train for Livorno two days before the ship was to leave. That would allow them to board the ship and get settled before setting sail.

At the dock Maria looked up in amazement at the three masted schooner she was about to board, the *Elizabeth*. She had never seen such a big boat. They were taken to their quarters in the stern and introduced to the Captain, Captain Seth Hasty and his wife Catherine. Maria and Margaret both had big smiles as they entered their large, comfortable rooms adjacent to the Captain's quarters. There was even a small parlor and dining area between their rooms. A crib had been found for Nino. The voyage was about to begin on a positive note.

The first night on board, while still in port, they dined with the Captain and his wife and the meal was surprisingly good. When the Captain discovered Charles was a sculptor he told him their cargo was silk, olive oil, and one hundred and fifty tons of marble. They even had a sculpture by an artist in Florence bound for Charleston, South Carolina.

They woke in the morning of May 17 to the sounds of the crew preparing the ship to depart. Charles and Ossoli were fascinated by the activity on the deck. The crew consisted of a first mate, second mate, fifteen sailors, a cook, and cabin boy. The first and second mates moved about the deck shouting orders to the sailors who unfurled the sails on the three masts. Nino giggled when he heard the rustling and sharp cracking of the sails as they filled with wind.

Two hours later they were ready to push off. More shouting of orders to the crew heaving thick mooring lines off to dock hands and they were on their way. The four stood along the rail watching as the ship moved from the dock and began maneuvering out of the harbor. As the shore faded from sight Maria once again wondered if she would ever return to Italy again.

All four were soon sea sick. Only Nino adjusted to the continual rocking rhythm as the ship cut through the waves and deep swells of the sea. After about four days of misery they began to improve, but Maria would never forget the feeling. It was as bad as she had been told. Luckily, they had favorable winds and were making good progress.

Six days out Captain Hasty didn't join the group for meals. His wife said he was in bed complaining of muscle aches, a fever, and puffiness of his eyes. The next day she informed them he had a rash that looked like small pox. They were all terrified. The Captain had held and played with Nino and had dined with them every day. Ossoli insisted on seeing the rash for himself, and when he returned informed them there was no question it was small pox.

Seven days out they anchored in the harbor of Gibraltar, Spain. Captain Hasty died during the night and the next day was buried at sea. The ship and all on board were quarantined by the harbor master for seven days and the ship had to be dusted with sulphur powder.

Everyone was nervous. Small pox was highly contagious for adults and more so for children. The women would not leave Nino out of their sight, checking his skin every hour and watching for any sign of a fever. At the end of the quarantine no one on the ship became sick and First Mate Bangs took over as Captain. They were cleared to sail.

Two days out from Gibraltar, Nino developed a fever and the following day the typical lesions of small pox covered his skin. Margaret became frantic. Captain Bangs would not return to Gibraltar and when Ossoli threatened him, he argued they would again be quarantined and this time no one would be allowed aboard for two weeks.

Maria knew Margaret was too upset to be of any help and cared for Nino. Everyone was relieved when the small pox lesions began to fade in two days and were gone in a week. Another miracle thought Charles. He wondered if Ossoli was thinking the same thing.

They reached Bermuda on July 14. Three days later, as they sailed along the eastern shore of America the wind began to get stromger. By the next day the wind velocity approached gale force and the waves became higher, making it dangerous to be on deck. Maria once again became seasick. That night as they lay in bed, Charles couldn't sleep. The rough rolling sea and roaring wind intensified making it impossible to lay still.

About four in the morning on July19, a sudden powerful jolt and abrupt halt to the movement of the ship threw Charles and Maria from their bed. He heard a brief loud scraping sound coming from the bottom of the hull and then the ship rolled over to one side and did not right itself. It all happened suddenly.

Maria screamed. Dazed, Charles looked around the room now at a fixed odd angle. He crawled to Maria and took her in his arms, trying to calm her. "What happened Charles, are we sinking?"

"I'm not sure, but I don't think we're sinking. We hit something. You stay where you are, I'll see if I can find out what happened."

Charles crawled to the door, but when he attempted to open it, it would not budge. He pounded on the door hoping someone outside would hear him. There was no response. He began kicking the door until it opened enough for him to see out into the darkness. All he could see were the huge waves pounding the ship, now lying on its side.

He crawled back to Maria and shouted, "We've run aground. We're not sinking, but we'll have to get off the ship. These powerful waves will destroy it. See if you can find your clothes and I'll try to open the door."

Charles found his pants and purse, threw the strap over his shoulder, and returned to the door. He doubted he could open it without an ax. The frame must have twisted when the boat hit land, jamming the door. As he was struggling to open it the blade of an ax came crashing through the door-panel almost hitting Charles's hand. He rolled back and watched as a crewman finished chopping a large opening in the door.

"Follow me," shouted the crewman.

Charles crawled back to get Maria and shouted, "I want you to hold my hand as tight as you can. Never let go. We're going to move to a safer part of the boat. Waves will be crashing over the side and may knock us down."

They left the cabin and crawling and sliding on the slippery deck between the collapsed sails and shattered masts followed the crewman. The huge waves hitting the deck knocked them down repeatedly, but Maria never let go of Charles's hand and they made it to the bow of the boat and the forecastle, where the crew quarters remained undamaged. Charles looked back and could see the waves were already beginning to shatter the captain's quarters and their room.

Catching her breath, Maria looked around the room and when she saw their friends, ran to embrace Margaret and the baby. "I'm so confused," said Maria. "What's happened?"

"We hit a sandbar," said Captain Bangs.

"Where are we?" asked Charles.

"Off the coast of New York. I'm not sure where," answered the Captain. "We'll have to abandon ship. The hull is damaged and taking on water."

"How can we get to shore with all these huge waves?" asked Ossoli.

"We can't launch lifeboats into this sea. We need a line from the shore. It's almost dawn and we'll get a better idea of our situation when we can see the shore," said the Captain.

The door opened and a drenched crewman entered and reported, "I can see people on the shore. They tried to fire a line with a line mortar, but the wind is too strong and it got nowhere. We're about one hundred yards from shore."

"We can't launch a boat into this rough sea," said the Captain. "We have to make other plans."

"Why can't we wait until the storm passes over," suggested Charles. "And then make our way to shore or wait until they can launch boats to rescue us?"

"I'm afraid this is more than a storm. It has all the signs of a hurricane and the worst is yet to come. The stern is already breaking apart and when the hurricane arrives the damaged hull will be destroyed," said the Captain. "The ship will be a total wreck."

"What should we do?" asked Ossoli.

"There's wood scattered over the deck from the damaged masts and rope from the collapsed rigging. We can make planks, tie the passengers to the planks, and let the waves carry them into shore. One of the crew can go with each passenger," said the Captain.

"I can't leave my baby," cried a panic-stricken Margaret.

Ossoli tried to console her, but it only made her clutch Nino tighter.

"You and Maria should go now before the sea becomes even rougher," said Ossoli.

Charles did not know how to respond. If this was a hurricane, as the Captain suspected, they would all die as the ship broke to pieces. The idea of the plank sounded dangerous, but since they couldn't get a line to the ship from shore, it might be the only way to survive. Swimming would be impossible in these waves.

"Please go," said Margaret. "Don't wait for us. We must find a different way to get to the beach."

"I'll leave the ship last and will help the Ossolis," said the Captain.

Maria's eyes filled with tears. She felt so impotent. She and Margaret looked at each other helplessly and knew there was no perfect answer for this tragic dilemma. Charles and Ossoli embraced and Maria and Margaret cried in each other's arms.

In the first light of day, Charles could see people on the shore, but they showed no sign of preparing for an attempted rescue. Instead, they were inspecting the cargo already washed ashore from the damaged hull. He waved at them frantically, but they paid no attention. It was clear they were not about to risk their lives trying to face the huge waves crashing on the shore.

Charles and a crewman made a plank. When they finished tying Maria to it, Charles said he would go with Maria, not the crewman. He would be tied to a line from the plank.

When ready to be launched, they looked at each other and wondered if they would ever see each other again. Now. he thought would be a good time to pray, before shouting to the crew, "We're ready."

They hit the water in a trough between two waves and floated upward toward the crest of the following wave where the plank tumbled out of control banging into Charles's body He lost sight of Maria. The chaotic ride continued toward the beach until Charles was slammed into shallow water by the force of the waves. Instinctively he grasped the rope attached to the plank and pulled with all the strength he had left.

Maria, was choking and spitting up water. He ran to her as fast as he could and dragged the plank to shore away from the crashing waves. When he loosened the ropes, she sat up, bent forward, continued to cough, and vomited more water. Charles picked her up and carried her farther from the shore. Then, exhausted, both collapsed on the sand.

Maria was the first to sit up. It was light, but a great dark cloud hovered over the water. The waves were even higher and the wind stronger, driving the accompanying rain horizontal with such force she had to shield her face and eyes with her hands. She looked back into the wind as best she could. The ship was on its side and breaking apart. She could see no one on the wreck of the ship, and scanning the beach did not see Margaret, Ossoli, or the baby. A young man came running over and said, "Are you all right? I'm one of the crew who made it."

"Did you see the Ossolis and their baby?" pleaded Maria.

"No ma'am, I've not seen them. You're the only passengers I've seen. Not even Captain Bangs made it."

She remembered he was the last one of the crew remaining when they left and if he didn't make it, Ossoli, Margaret, and Nino must not have either. Charles began to sit up and she rushed to embrace him repeating over and over through her tears, "They're gone, they're gone, and the baby's gone. How horrible."

They stayed in each other's arms a long time, both in shock. They were interrupted by a woman who tugged Maria's arm and said, "Follow me. We have to get off this beach because there may be a surge of water flooding this beach as the hurricane passes over. We must get inland to be safe."

The strong wind and thick brush made it difficult to walk as they followed her inland to a small run-down house. As soon as they walked through the door they were welcomed by the warmth of a small fire-place and shelter from the wind and rain. The woman made coffee before asking them where their ship was headed. Charles told her about the trip and asked where they were. When the woman told them they had hit a sandbar off Fire Island, Long Island, they wondered how Captain Bangs had wandered so far off course.

"Why didn't anyone try to help us?" asked Charles.

"You're not the first ship to hit a sand bar in the shallow water surrounding this island. Ships get off course in the dark and there are sand bars everywhere. The only difference with your ship was the hurricane. I haven't seen such a storm in years. The few people who live around here know the ocean and fear it. They knew they would have no chance of launching small boats into the wind and waves of this hurricane.

"We tried to fire a line to the boat with a mortar, but the wind was too strong," said the woman. "You can stay here tonight. All I have to offer is the floor by the fireplace. The hurricane should have passed over by tomorrow. Then we can get you on your way to New York. I'll let the man who lives down the road know you need to get to the city. He can take you to the ferry."

The wind continued to increase creating a terrifying noise. Charles and Maria huddled together, certain the tiny house would be blown apart. After about three hours the wind and noise began to decrease, but the rain persisted, and even became heavier. By this time Charles and Maria, both exhausted, fell asleep in each other's arms.

———

The next morning Charles's body ached from the pounding it took by the wooden plank. Outside, the wind had died, the sky was clear and the ocean calm. It was hard to believe after how fierce the wind of the hurricane had been the night before. They walked back to the beach to look for other survivors. They found none. Maria gasped when she saw the ship, now a total wreck, a pile of disjointed wood with scattered hints of the former structure surrounding its cargo of marble, the only thing capable of withstanding the fury of the hurricane.

Both stopped when they saw a portable desk partially embedded in the sand at the shore line. Maria ran to it shouting, "That's Margaret's. I'd know it anywhere. It was her most treasured possession." It was intact except for the lock on the top drawer. Someone had broken it off and the drawer was hanging half open.

Then she pointed to scattered sheets of papers on the sand and floating in the shallow water. She dashed into the water to retrieve them and walked around the beach picking up additional loose sheets. They found more papers in the desk. "These are important. Margaret was writing a history of the revolution in Rome and the struggle for unification of Italy," said Maria.

"We must get these to her family in Boston. I learned so much from her and admired her brilliance. Italy's greatest patriot and intellectual, Mazzini, came to her to discuss his ideas. She showed me what a woman can be. Many men feared her or dismissed her because they discovered they were dealing with their equal or better and prejudice would not allow them to accept such a woman. Now, here I am, an uneducated woman from the mountains of Italy, picking up the final pieces of her extraordinary life."

"We both have lost so much," added Charles. "Let's see if we can get this desk to her family in Boston. It may not be easy."

He was right. There were few people living on this island. The roads were more like trails and he had no idea where to find a ferry to take them to the mainland. They didn't even find their trunks washed up on the beach. Their only possession that survived was his purse, the strap still over his shoulder.

A stranger approached them and asked, "Are you the two who need to get to the city?"

"Yes, where do we go?' answered Charles.

"I'll get you there. Do you have any money?"

"Yes, I do," said Charles. When does it leave?"

"This afternoon. I see you have that box. Are you taking that? If you are It'll cost more. You're lucky its summer because the ferry don't run during the winter." Having no other choice, Charles paid the man his outrageous price.

The primitive ferry struggled to cross the water leaving Maria to wonder if they would make it to the other shore. They landed in a small village of wooden, weather-worn buildings, all showing damage from last night's hurricane.

Walking down the single rain-soaked mud street, both barefooted, Charles saw a small sign on one building identifying it as a Saloon and Inn. When they entered the wife of the owner made them stop until she could find a cloth for them to clean their feet. Both jumped at the opportunity. As they cleaned the mud from their feet the owner walked over and asked, "What boat were you on?"

"The *Elizabeth*," answered Charles.

"Lost everything, haven't you?" he asked. "It's not the first time I've had survivors stay here and it won't be the last time. It takes an experienced Captain to avoid the sandbars."

Charles and Maria looked woefully at each other, knowing they would never forget their trip with the inexperienced Captain Bangs making his first, and last transatlantic voyage.

"We have a room. Do you have any money?" asked the owner.

"Yes," said Charles.

"Good. I think we can even get you some new clothes at the general store. We'll get you to New York city. That's where you were going wasn't it?"

"Yes, thank you," said Charles, who almost said *grazie*.

When they entered their room, both fell onto the bed and Maria said, "Hold me tight. I can't believe what happened to us. The storm, losing Margaret, Ossoli, and Nino. Tell me it was a bad dream."

"Wish I could. I think it'll be a long time before we recover from this horror. All we can do now is be grateful for our survival."

"Before we go any further I want you to promise you'll write a letter to Margaret's family telling them what happened. We have to be certain they get her desk and all the papers. We can get the address of the family from the *New York Tribune*, where Margaret sent all her dispatches."

"I agree, we'll ship everything to the family before we go on to Washington," said Charles.

Requesting the address of Margaret's family at the *New York Tribune* caused an unexpected disturbance in the newsroom. Suddenly Charles and Maria were surrounded by reporters deluging them with questions about the shipwreck. Finally, a man walked up to the reporters surrounding them and they all backed away. "Sorry for the trouble they've caused. We've had no luck discovering what happened to Margaret Fuller and were told there were no survivors of the shipwreck. I'm the assistant editor and understand you were with her on the *Elizabeth*," said the man as he led them to his office. "Wait here while I get the editor, Mr. Horace Greely."

They spent the rest of the afternoon being interviewed by the editor. When they first mentioned Ossoli's name he had no idea who they meant. He was even more surprised when they mentioned Nino and they answered more questions about the relationship between Margaret and Ossoli than the details of the shipwreck. At the end of the lengthy interview Greely agreed to ship Margaret's desk and papers to her family in Boston and pay the Grimes's hotel bill.

Walking back to their hotel, Maria said, "Margaret was even more important than we knew. They were surprised to know she had married Ossoli. I remember she never talked about marriage, but I always took it for granted they were married. They were so in love."

"Ossoli told me they were married. It isn't important now though, is it?"

"No," said Maria, "It isn't."

Maria was having a hard time understanding New York. Wood instead of stone was the choice of building material for almost everything including churches that looked plain and uninviting. There was no wall around the city that seemed to spread out haphazardly in every direction.

The streets were wider and in the center of the city paved with bricks, but, outside the center, many streets were dirt, and a few covered with wood planks. People were in constant motion and few stopped to talk with one another. She would not want to live here.

The next day they left for Washington. During the train ride Maria quizzed Charles nonstop about his two brothers and two sisters, the mother, and father. Would they like her? He kept reassuring her they would, but the closer they came to Washington the more anxious she became.

He had been away five years, and was eager to see his family. They were modest people who kept a loving home and grateful with what life had brought them. But he was not the same innocent young man who left for Rome to study sculpture. What he had experienced there the last four years had to have changed him. Would they notice?

Their trunks were lost in the shipwreck and their luggage now consisted of a small suitcase filled a few clothes purchased in New York and a gift for his mother. They hired a carriage outside the train station in Washington and, as they rode through the streets Maria was again puzzled by this strange new country, America.

In this city of about forty thousand, compared to the five hundred thousand in New York, the streets were dirt and lined by plain wooden houses separated from each other by grass and gardens. Multistoried buildings, up to four floors, with shops on the ground level filled the center of the city. Wooden sidewalks lined the front of the shops. At one-point Maria could see a large stone building with a central dome and asked, "Is that your Duomo?"

"No," Charles said, laughing, "It's the Capitol building, like the building for the Chamber of deputies in Rome or the Quirinal for the Pope."

"Is there a piazza in front of it? I don't see any piazzas. Where do the people gather?"

"There are no piazzas and no walls around the city. Settlers have been in this country since the seventeenth century, but the United States is only about sixty-five years old. Rome has been in existence for over two thousand years. This Capitol and its surrounding buildings are only fifty years old, and don't forget Italy is still fighting to form a unified country, so we'll be older than your new unified country. If and when that happens."

"It will," said Maria sharply as the carriage stopped at a small frame house with a picket fence in front.

"Here we are. Just as I remember it."

It didn't take long before his mother came running from the house shouting, "Charles is here! Father did you hear me? Charles is here!"

After an absence of five years the reunion was a mix of joy and tears. Between numerous hugs and kisses his mother said, "We thought you were dead. You wrote us you were sailing on the *Elizabeth* and the newspaper said it sank off Long Island and there were no survivors. Oh, my goodness, your wife. I forgot. I'm embarrassed. Maria welcome to America, but you can understand. We've been mourning your loss, but here you are. Almost too much to grasp." She reached out to help Maria down from the carriage.

His father left to let the others in the family know Charles and his wife were not dead, but here in Washington. Within an hour they were all gathered at the house listening to Charles tell of the wreck of the *Elizabeth* and their survival. Everyone, including his nieces and nephews, some born after he left, were enthralled by his story of their adventure.

Maria's anxieties concerning acceptance by his parents and family were short-lived. They were excited to have a new daughter and sister-in-law and the children were in awe of their new aunt with the charming accent from a faraway land across the ocean.

The next few days were spent becoming further acquainted with his parents and family. When the excitement over his return finally waned, Charles and Maria were at last able to rest. They slept ten to twelve hours for three consecutive days. His mother became concerned, but he convinced her they were not sick, only physically and emotionally exhausted from their life-threatening experience.

Once rested Charles was anxious to see if there had been any progress in the past four years on the government buildings. He also wanted to meet the senator from Maryland who told him about the need for American sculptors. What impressed him most was how much the city had grown in the five years he'd been away.

The Capitol was completed when he left and there was nothing new to be seen there, at least on the exterior. It was the surrounding area that was changing. The National Botanic Garden had expanded, including

filling in much of the swamp where it had been located. A new building, that looked like a brick castle, called the Smithsonian Institute, was
almost completed. He didn't see any need for marble sculptors there at
this time, but decided he should still stop to see the senator.

The senator greeted him warmly and said, "I remember our conversation in Florence. Welcome home."

"It's nice to be back and see my family," said Charles. "The city is
growing fast and I see there's new construction around the Capitol."

"Yes, and more to come. That's what I meant when I told you we
needed American sculptors."

"There wasn't much marble or sculpture in the current construction I saw."

"No, but there will be. The architectural competition for the expansion of the Capitol has ended. There were five finalists and President
Fillmore is about to select the one architect who will be in charge of
the expansion. I've seen all the drawings submitted. No matter who is
selected this will be a massive project that will take at least five years."

"When will construction begin?"

"This summer. Powers told me you are a good sculptor and know
how to work with people, particularly marble carvers. This will also
be an opportunity to train American marble carvers. We have marble
quarries in America. They also need work."

"It's not clear to me. Are you looking for a sculptor, or some sort
of supervisor for the expansion project?"

"Both, someone who can not only add his artistic touch to the
work, but also supervise these Italian carvers we now have. They refuse
to train Americans and with no competition they can be annoyingly
independent. They're paid a good wage, but are taking advantage of
the situation and making unreasonable demands."

"And the work will be starting this summer?".

"Yes. Let me take you to meet President Fillmore. He's tired of
hearing congressman complain about importing Italians to work on
the Capitol. The pay would be excellent."

"Thank you. Let me think about it," answered Charles.

"Young man this is a great opportunity. I'll be waiting anxiously for your answer," said the senator.

Walking home Charles felt enthusiastic about the offer and had to agree the guarantee of steady work and good salary was hard to turn down. He would be living close to his family and participate in the rapid growth occurring in Washington. He would be foolish not to give the offer serious consideration.

He thought about it for a week before telling Maria. On a warm pleasant Sunday afternoon while lying in the grass in the shade of a large oak tree in the back yard of his parent's home he said, "Thank you for becoming close to my parents. It's apparent they like you."

"And I like them," said Maria. "You know how I've missed being part of a family and now, once again I have one."

"I want to talk to you about something. I've had an offer of a good job here. They'll be building extensions to our Duomo," laughed Charles, "as you refer to it. This project will take at least five years. I'd be supervising the work of the marble carvers and advising on any other construction of the extensions requiring marble as the building material. The pay is good and we would have a steady income. What do you think?"

"How did they find you?"

"I met a senator who was visiting Powers's studio in Florence and he recommended me."

"You said nothing about your own work being part of the project."

"That's a possibility, but nothing specific yet."

"You know I'd never stand in the way of any decision you make. You've become successful on the merits of your work. You know best what you want to accomplish. I also have something to tell you."

"What"

"I'm going to have a baby."

Charles was speechless. He rolled over, kissed her, and asked, "You're sure?"

"I am, Maria blushed. "Your mother could tell without even asking me.?

"When do you think you'll have the baby?"

"I think February, perhaps early March. I figure I became with child while we were sailing across the Atlantic."

"And the baby survived the shipwreck. You're a strong woman. We're lucky you didn't lose the baby."

"We are. Does this effect your decision?"

"No and yes— I know you'll support any decision I make, but from now on we'll have a family to consider. I have to think about this again. What a great surprise. If it's a boy I think we should call him Piero. What do you think?"

"That's a good idea. I like the name Piero. If it's a girl, I get to pick the name."

Charles laid back in the grass and watching the summer clouds passing overhead and thought about this pleasant surprise about to change their lives. He wanted a family, but this was unexpected. He hadn't considered that in making his decision. Working on the construction of the Capitol extensions answered the many insecurities associated with being a sculptor, but on the other hand he already had money in banks both in America and Rome.

He would be working for the architect chosen by the President and didn't knowwho it would be. It could be a way to develop contacts that could lead to commissions, but would there be time to do outside work? He knew little about architecture. The Italian carvers would see him as a threat to their jobs and could be difficult to manage.

He was a sculptor. That was the world he knew and loved. Being the only American sculptor in this developing city, lacking any hint of artistic sophistication, would be lonely. The marble, the carvers, mold makers, tool makers, tourist clients, and on and on. It was all there in

Rome. He would have to recreate that world here, leaving him little time to do his own work.

He loved his family in America, but since marrying Maria his life had taken a different course. Fighting the French with the Civic Guard changed him. His acceptance in their Rome neighborhood and by his carvers for the risk he had taken meant a great deal to him. Maria had introduced him to a world of love he never knew existed. But he remembered what Piero had said about the uprising in Rome last year. It was probably only the beginning of a long struggle to unify Italy. A struggle that could disrupt everyone's life in the Eternal City.

Instead he could become an important figure in the evolution of the capital of America. He pictured all the magnificent buildings in Rome. Why couldn't we build a capital here to rival the great cities of Athens and Rome? It was not unheard of for sculptors to contribute their talents to the planning and construction of buildings. Michelangelo often did.

There were lots of 'ifs' in this proposal. He would be taking a chance, a risk that could hurt his career, but he felt the same insecurity before he decided to go to Rome. Even more so. And look how far that had taken his career.

Still looking up at the clouds he said to Maria, "I've decided. I'm going to take this job in Washington." Charles could not see, but she had a big smile. With child, and distant from the ancient traditions of her mountain culture, it was time for her to pursue her own dreams in this new world.

Author's Notes

Researching the life of Thomas Crawford, the sculptor of *Statue of Freedom* on the Capitol Dome in Washington DC, I discovered he had enlisted in the Civic Guard in Rome, as did several other young American sculptors studying there at the same time as this story. It seemed like an interesting subject for a book.

The Caffé Greco existed then as it does now, on Via dei Condotti. A letter from Mazzini was thrown into Pio Nono's carriage as described in the story. The description of Pellegrino Rossi's murder is based on an article in the English newspaper in Rome at that time, *The Roman Advertiser. A Journal of Italian Intelligence, Science, Literature, and Fine Arts*, November 18, 1848.

The demonstrations described in the piazzas are based on actual events. Ciceruacchio (Angelo Brunetti), was a popular supporter of Pio Nono and, some accounts say his son stabbed Pellegrino Rossi, but another person was later tried and convicted of the murder. After he left Rome with Garibaldi, Ciceruacchio was captured and shot by the Austrians, along with his sons, Lorenzo and Angelo.

The proclamation of the *National Popular Club of Rome* and the decree establishing the Roman Republic, were both taken from the newspaper, *The Roman Advertiser*, noted above.

Margaret Fuller and Marchese Giovanni Angelo Ossoli met when she became separated from her friends at the basilica of St Peter. Fuller left her baby with a wet nurse in Rieti, and the question of whether Fuller and Ossoli ever married was for a long time unanswered, but later confirmed by records in Rieti.

The dates of the sieges of Rome by the French are accurate. A major storm did interfere with the final day of the French siege.

Captain Hasty of the *Elizabeth* died of smallpox and Nino also contracted the disease, but recovered.

There was a hurricane along the East Coast of the United States on the date noted, and there are different accounts of the shipwreck at Point O' Woods, Fire Island, New York. The bodies of Margaret Fuller and Ossoli were never found. Nino's body was found and buried in a trunk on the beach, but later recovered by Fuller's family. Ralph Waldo Emerson persuaded Henry Thoreau (also a friend of Fuller) to go to Fire island to investigate the shipwreck. Six islanders were arrested for plundering the *Elizabeth*, but it is unclear if they were ever convicted of any crime. The crate containing the sculpture of Senator Calhoun was recovered later by a diver at the scene of the wreck of the *Elizabeth*.

Giuseppe Garibaldi fled to America in 1850, but later returned to Italy to join the final struggle to unify the northern and southern kingdoms of Italy. His reputation as a warrior even caught the interest of President Abraham Lincoln, who early in the Civil War, sent an envoy to convince him to train Lincoln's generals in guerilla warfare. Garibaldi declined the invitation.

Italian troops seized Rome on September 1870 ending Pio Nono's temporal rule of the Papal States. King Victor Emmanuel II established Rome as the capital of the unified Italy in July 1871. Pio Nono continued his papacy until his death in 1878, the longest reign of any pope.

Giuseppe Mazzini lived to see the unification of the kingdoms of Italy and died in Pisa, Italy in 1872.

About the Author

Richard F Novak is a physician and sculptor with an interest in the American neoclassical sculptors who studied in Rome and Florence in the nineteenth century. He has spent a year of his life traveling throughout Italy studying the works of the Italian sculptors. There are over seventy-five of his own works in public spaces, corporate, and private collections. His books always incorporate a background of sculpture or sculptors. Examples of Novak's sculpture can be seen in the Photo Gallery section of *toppingthedome.com*.

Made in the USA
Middletown, DE
18 April 2021